A Horse Called Gem

Jenny Hughes

A Horse Called Gem

ISBN 82 591 0868 2

Chapter One

I always think galloping is like flying. It gives you the same sense of speed and power and the same breathtaking feel of excitement. My second eldest brother, who doesn't ride, says that's silly because, as he puts it, "horses don't even go as fast as cars, so how can you compare them with airplanes?" But he's missing the point. It's the feeling, that glorious sensation when your pony lengthens his stride and races joyfully across the ground, neck outstretched, mane and tail streaming like victory banners.

It was just like that the morning we met Mary. Jack and I had been out for over an hour. Our ponies, Cody and Gem, were nicely warmed up and raring to go, so when we saw our favorite trail sloping gently upwards across the hillside we couldn't resist it. To be honest, I started it. Cody is so fast, Gem and I have to be a little sneaky if we're going to have any chance of getting our nose in front. We were already cantering fairly sedately, but when I gave my horribly loud impression of an Apache war cry – you know, "yee hah, yow, yow, YOW!" – Gem plunged straight into

a flat-out gallop. For a few wonderful moments we were in the lead, then Cody was beside us, nostrils flaring as he forged easily ahead. Jack was laughing his head off. He's always telling me I should warn him when Gem and I are going to do something a little crazy, but he and his horse enjoy it as much as we do.

As usual, my handsome gray pony did his best to catch Cody, and I kept whooping and howling, partly because it spurs Gem on and partly because it's fun. Jack was yelling childish things like, "Can't catch me!" and "What's the matter Billie, got your brakes on?" and we really were making a whole lot of noise. It's never been a problem before, since there's hardly ever anybody around on our remote stretch of the foothills, but that day was different. As Jack crested the top of the hill he suddenly saw a lone rider on an elegant-looking black horse, just in front of him. He held up his hand to slow me down but I was so intent on trying to catch up I didn't see it. I was still screeching too, I'm afraid, and by the time I saw the black horse the damage had been done.

We were still a little ways behind him, but I watched him turn his head towards us, saw the panicky gleam in his eye and knew he was going to bolt. If he'd just gone in a straight line it wouldn't have been too bad, because the trail goes gently uphill again and is very safe, but to my horror he veered nervously to the left. The rider, a girl whose blonde hair was tumbling from under her hat, gave a frightened squeak, then lost one stirrup and her grip on the reins, as her horse galloped wildly heading straight towards the cliff edge a few hundred yards away.

"Jack!" I yelled, but he'd already spun Cody and was following. The black horse's stride seemed impossibly long

7

as he flew across the turf and Cody, who was smaller, had to gallop flat out to draw level. Jack was calling to the girl, telling her to stop hauling on both reins and instead "give and take" with her offside to try and slow him. Gradually Cody drew ahead of the panicking horse, and I was relieved to see that both ponies were slowing down and, more importantly, Jack was heading them away from the dangerous edge of the cliff.

I drew in a huge gulp of air. I'd been so worried I think I forgot to breathe for those few minutes. Jack's bay pony, now in a collected canter, was leading the other horse back to safety, and I watched them come to a halt on the broad trail ahead. The blonde girl still seemed to be shocked and frightened. Jack gallantly stood and held her horse for her as she slithered to the ground where she sank, rather melodramatically I thought, to lie prone on the grass. Jack looked helplessly in my direction, and I moved Gem towards them at a sedate walk so we wouldn't spook the black horse again. I was really, genuinely sorry we'd nearly caused a terrible accident with our clowning around and, as soon as I reached the girl, I blurted out a very embarrassed apology.

"It wasn't your fault," the fair-haired girl said as she raised her tear-stained face. "I should be able to hold Solace but when we're out here, he's too strong for me."

"No, no it was us, wasn't it, Jack?" I looked at him and he shuffled his feet.

"Yes it was. We shouldn't have been so wild. Sorry."

"It's OK, honestly." She had a soft voice with a distinct English accent.

"You're from England, aren't you?" I said brightly, hoping to stop her crying. "We're both from around here,

I'm Billie and he's Jack. The flying bay is called Cody and my gorgeous pony is Gem."

"I'm pleased to meet you. It's so nice to find someone friendly." She still looked sad but at least the tears had stopped flowing. "My name's Mary and this fellow is called Solace. We came over from England a week or two ago and are living at Longrigg House."

"Cool!" I was impressed. Longrigg is a big country mansion set in fabulous grounds a mile or two outside our town. "I thought there was only a crazy old man there," I added tactlessly, and Mary gave her first tentative smile.

"I expect you mean my uncle, or great-uncle, I suppose he was. He died some time ago and my cousin Paul owns it now."

I wanted to know more but Jack butted in quickly, obviously not feeling the same way.

"Yeah well, we'll ride with you to the house, just in case Solace takes off again. Then we'll head for home ourselves."

Mary thanked him and then spent ages fiddling around, first with her hat and then Solace's girth, while Jack stood there trying not to look irritated. Jack hates it when people fuss around and don't just get on with their riding. Once Mary was finally aboard, he swung easily into Cody's saddle and muttered quietly to me, "We leave her at Longrigg's gate and don't offer to see her again. She is such as wimp!"

I thought it was true but a little unkind. To make up for Jack being so stand-offish, I babbled away to Mary as we rode quietly along the trail leading off the hills. She was nearly fourteen, she told me, and had only ever been to America on a vacation.

"But this time I'm here to stay, or at least I hope I am,"

she went on and, to my surprise, tears welled up in her eyes again.

"Oh, don't cry." I'm a total softie when it comes to people weeping. "What's the matter?"

"You don't want to hear my problems." She tried to smile, and I felt so sorry for her I immediately said, "Of course we do. Don't we, Jack?"

He gave me a dirty look, very different from his usual grin, the one that makes my knees turn to jelly when I think about it.

"Perhaps Mary doesn't want to tell us," he said pointedly.

"It'll do her good," I retorted and trotted Gem close enough to Solace for me to reach out and pat Mary's hand encouragingly. "And after the scare we gave her it's the least we can do."

"You're very kind, Billie," she brushed the tears away. "I'm sure if I had someone like you on my side I could get to grips with everything."

"Fire away!" I was being very upbeat. "Tell us your troubles."

Once she started talking it seemed she couldn't stop and Jack and I listened in horror. Both her parents had been killed in a car crash in England and, after months of lawyers arguing about guardianship, Mary had been brought across the Atlantic to stay with her only living relative, her mother's cousin, Paul.

"Paul is really nice, a lovely guy, but he's got problems of his own. I don't like to bother him with mine."

"So bother us instead." I was feeling more and more sorry for her.

She hesitated. "I – I won't tell you about the really big problem we have but – well the trouble I'm trying to deal with on my own is about Solace, and you two seem to know rather a lot about horses."

"We're pretty good, aren't we Jack?" I grinned at him encouragingly, and he gave a reluctant smile. I could see he still didn't really want to get involved, but although he likes to act all tough and macho, he's very kind-hearted under-neath.

"Not bad." he said warily. "What sort of trouble do you mean, Mary?"

"Um, I guess most of it's down to me being nervous, but I'm sure I could manage if it wasn't for Kyle."

"Kyle?" Jack put in harshly. "Not Kyle Pritchard?"

"Oh you know him? In which case you can tell me if he's as horrible to everyone else. Virtually every time Solace and I have been out for a hack, Kyle and some creepy-looking older guy have done everything they can to spoil our ride."

"The older one would be Kyle's new groom," I said to Jack. "There have already been two or three who have quit the job."

"Anyone in their right mind would," said Jack. His dark, good-looking face was grim. "Kyle ruins the poor horses his dad buys for him. He's got hands like cement shovels and he uses his stick to force his horse into obeying him."

"Jack took Kyle's whip and broke it over his head after one cross-country event," I told Mary, and her face broke into the first real smile we'd seen.

"I'd have paid to see that! You see he knows I've only ever lived in the city and all my riding's been done in a ring. I've won cups with Solace, he's absolutely brilliant at show jumping, but he's never been out in open country like this. Kyle deliberately chases us to scare Solace into bolting or gets him to spook just as we're about to jump a ditch. That's

11

the problem I don't want to bother Paul with. Today was the fifth time I've been chased down, and I'm getting more and more scared to come out."

"I'm so sorry," I said again, deeply ashamed that she'd probably thought it was the detestable Kyle when we came screaming up behind her. "We've just made things worse for you."

"No you haven't. Jack's tip on how to slow Solace down was a big help." She hesitated. "I don't suppose you'd be able to give me any more advice?"

I looked at Jack. He'd been pretty definite about not seeing her again.

"You can come out with us sometime if you like," he said reluctantly. "It's really just a matter of time, getting you and Solace used to the great outdoors and building up your confidence in each other again. Once he's completely relaxed and under your control you can start enjoying a good gallop like we do. There's no rush."

"Oh but there is!" Mary's lips were set in a surprisingly firm line. "I keep meeting Kyle in Longrigg Wood, you know, that pretty stretch of country outside our walls. He keeps chasing me off and calling me names like 'prissy miss' and 'scary Mary' and…"

"What a pig!" I'd always thought Kyle was arrogant but this was really out of line. "We'll come with you next time you ride in the woods. He won't be so brave with Jack around."

"Good idea, but like I said, let's take it slowly. You've got a lot to get used to." Jack gave his fabulous grin, which made me melt, but it didn't seem to have much effect on Mary.

"I can't take it slowly." She turned from him and looked

12

at me imploringly. "Because I couldn't stand Kyle calling me a coward all the time, I said I'd show him by beating him at the next competition he's going in for. It was my way of telling him he can't frighten me, but I didn't realize there's a Hunter Trial in just a couple of weeks. I've gotten so nervous about riding Solace out in the open that I'm never going to do it on my own. You will help me, won't you?"

Chapter Two

Jack and I looked at each other in dismay. I was the first to respond.

"Of course we will!" I tried to put some real enthusiasm into my voice. I just couldn't say no to someone who, after having their world fall apart, was now being run out of town by the local slimeball. Jack made a strangled sort of noise in his throat which I took for agreement, and I was quick to take advantage of it. "Um, maybe we should start by seeing what you and Solace can do in the ring. We have one at our yard but it's pretty booked up —"

"There's a paddock behind the stables at Longrigg." Mary looked so much better when she smiled. "I think that's a great idea, so will you come over tomorrow morning?"

I couldn't think of an excuse, so I smiled back and nodded, and Jack made the peculiar sound again. We'd reached the tall, wrought-iron gates of Longrigg House and Mary rode Solace up the curving drive, waving good-bye and looking 10 times happier.

"Great!" Jack said bitterly once she was out of sight. "I told you not to get involved and now look what you've done."

"Oh come on, Jack." I tried a winning smile on him but he just drew his black brows together in a scowl. "I couldn't just say 'No, tough luck, sorry we don't want to help you.' And besides the agony she's been through, we did almost send her over a cliff, so I think we owe her something!"

"But you saw what she was like! OK, we spooked her horse but she was hopeless, all teary and prissy, and such a cry-baby!"

Jack isn't used to cry-babies. I've got three older brothers who've made sure I've grown up very tough and capable. Of course I have my "girl" moments, but I've learned not to show any sign of being what they (and Jack) think of as wimpy. Jack and I have known each other forever. Our moms are best friends and the two of us were introduced 14 years ago, when I was just a few weeks old and Jack was three months. Of course I don't actually remember anything about that first meeting, but as we got older we both developed a passion for horses and riding and, for the past few years, we've been practically inseparable. Both our families live in ordinary houses with smallish yards so we keep Gem and Cody at a nice stable about a mile away. Jack comes over on his bike and gets me every morning, and we do our stable chores and put the ponies out in a paddock if it's a school day, or take them for a hack if it's vacation like now. I've already mentioned that Jack's bay pony, Cody, is as fast as lightning, but he doesn't jump as well as my beautiful dapple gray Gem, which balances us out nicely when it comes to competitions. We get along really well, and the ponies like each other too, so it had been pretty near perfect, I'd always thought. But now Mary had arrived and, instead of the four of us galloping carefree across the hills or leaping the homemade cross-country course in Longrigg Wood, we'd be spending our time trying to show a nervous, weepy English girl how to become a fearless event rider. I wasn't exactly delighted at the prospect myself, but I knew it had to be done.

I tried smiling at Jack again and, encouraged when he didn't scowl quite so hard, I said (in what I hoped were flattering tones), "Please help Mary anyway. If anybody can teach her it's you. You're so good at cross-country riding – look at what a great job you did with Gem and me."

"That's different," he said, turning his dark eyes towards me. "You're – you're sensible."

It wasn't exactly the nicest thing anyone's ever said to me, but I know he meant it as a compliment.

"Well, Mary's probably a lot better than she seemed," I argued. "She's been through a terrible time and I'll bet we've seen her at her worst. She must be tougher than she looks, coping with all her problems and still trying to stand up to that big bully Kyle."

"But what a thing to tell him!" Jack groaned. "She'll never be ready to compete in next month's Hunter Trial if she can't even stop Solace running off with her."

"But she told you your tip on stopping him helped a lot. I bet there's tons of advice you can give her," I said persuasively. "Oh please say you'll try, Jack."

"It doesn't look as though I have much choice, does it?" he grumbled, but the beginnings of a grin were there as he looked at me. "Fine. I'll do it. Only because it'll be fun to have a reason to chase scuzzbucket Kyle off."

"You'll enjoy that," I agreed happily. "I wonder why he's giving Mary such a hard time?"

"Because he's a jerk, and she's an easy target, I guess."

"There must be more to it than that," I said. "Maybe we'll find out in the next few days."

I knew once Jack had agreed to go through with helping Mary he'd stick to his word. The next morning we set off, turning left out of the yard gate instead of our usual right fork towards the hills.

"I've never been inside the grounds of Longrigg House, have you?" I asked him as we rode side-by-side along the quiet country lane.

"Yeah I have, just once. My mom took a bunch of us caroling there one Christmas. She thought it would cheer up the old man who was living there, but he refused to come out and just yelled through a window for us to get lost."

Jack had found that very funny but I thought it was sad.

"That would be her cousin Paul's father," I said, feeling a sudden shiver. "But he's gone now, and Mary says Paul is OK."

"He'd better be, I'm not putting up with a loony old miser *and* a drippy girl," Jack said firmly and we rode our ponies under the wrought iron arch and along the curving sweep of Longrigg's drive.

We were a little early, but Mary was already looking out for us, standing under a graceful silver birch tree and dressed in her riding gear. At her feet was the most gorgeous dog I'd ever seen, a cream and gray bundle of shaggy hair which fell over its eyes and cascaded from a fluffy, feathery tail curling over its back.

"Hi ya!" I called cheerfully and, as Mary waved, the dog's tail wagged even harder. "What a gorgeous dog!"

18

I hopped off Gem and bent down for a cuddle. "What's it called and what is it?"

"This is Maggie." Mary ruffled the dog's head affectionately, and I saw something sparkling through the hair. "She's a Tibetan Terrier – there's been one at Longrigg since my great aunt's days. Say hi to my friends, Maggie."

The dog immediately held out a shaggy paw, and I shook it solemnly.

"She's very pretty," I said admiringly, "And I do like the glamorous collar she's wearing. I hope those aren't real jewels."

"No, all the Longrigg dogs had rhinestone collars," Mary laughed. "It's all part of the traditional eccentricity, I guess."

"They sell them at the local pet store." Jack was grinning at Maggie. "I've seen a boxer wearing one but it didn't look as pretty as Maggie!"

"You don't mind if she comes with us?" Mary asked. "She's really taken to me since I arrived, she follows me everywhere. She won't be a nuisance."

"That's fine," Jack said "So, why don't you show us the way?"

We followed Mary and Maggie around the side of the big house and along a pathway and, as we turned the corner, Jack and I both let out a gasp. There was the most beautiful stable yard you'd ever seen, built of the same mellow stone as the house, with storerooms and big loose box stalls looking out onto a central courtyard. It was like a picture from a glossy magazine, it was so beautiful and so perfect.

"As you can see, Paul's already tidied up the stabling," said Mary, and walked to where Solace was tacked up, ready, and waiting in his stall. "He has two horses of his

own so he made sure everything was OK for them." She started leading her horse out.

"It's fabulous," I said, thinking of our humble wooden buildings. "Where are your cousin's horses now?"

"Paul's had to turn them out for the summer. He had a bad fall a few weeks ago and his leg still isn't mended so he can't ride. Solace will join them in the paddock once he's done his work this morning." She hesitated. "You're both very kind to help me like this. It must be a pain for you."

"Not at all," Jack said, lying through his teeth, "but let's get going. If we see what you can do in the ring we can talk about whether it's going to be possible for you to enter the Hunter Trial you mentioned."

"There's no question about it," Mary said sharply. "I've got to do it."

"OK, OK," I said peacefully. "Show us where your ring is."

We walked the horses round the back of the stable block to a very nice post-and-railed paddock, complete with dressage markers and real colored jumps. I stayed on Gem, walking him around to keep him warmed up, while Jack sat on the fence and put Mary and Solace through some flat work. Mary was surprisingly good, I thought, relaxed and supple with nice light hands and good balance. She looked completely different from the weepy, defeated girl who'd slumped in the saddle all the way home the day before. Jack asked for some lateral work, and Mary got Solace executing a perfect turn on the forehand, some leg yielding, shoulder in and half pass. I could tell from Jack's attitude that he was pleasantly surprised at how well she was doing and, when he asked her to pop the horse over a few poles, I knew he was happy with her riding abilities. Solace pricked his ears and approached the simple ascending oxer confidently, and Mary's technique was perfect. Jack went into the ring and changed the poles around, getting the pair to take the jumps in a different order, changing hands and sometimes putting a bounce stride between fences. I was itching to have a go on Gem and, at last, he took pity on me, and asked Mary if it was OK.

"Sure." She brought Solace out of the ring, and I trotted, then cantered Gem smoothly in varying figures of eight as he hopped over the jumps with his usual verve and style.

"Gosh, you two are good!" Mary said admiringly, and I thought maybe this wasn't going to be such a bad idea after all.

"So," Jack beckoned me over and I reluctantly left the paddock to join him and Mary. "Mary, we've established you can ride fine, which is great, now all you need is a bit of practice outside."

"I know that," she said impatiently. "That's what I told you. Solace and I have only ever worked indoors or in a ring like this. I mean, we've done some jumping outdoors but always in a fenced-off ring."

I stared at her. I just couldn't imagine it. To think she'd never cantered across the shallows of a river or galloped along a wide stretch of turf with the wind in her face, feeling the power and speed of her horse! Don't get me wrong, I know the benefits of good training, and I do my bit with Gem and take it seriously, but mostly my pony and I have lots and lots of outdoor fun. The really great thing about building Mary's confidence enough to ride Solace in the Hunter Trial is that they'd also be learning to relax and enjoy themselves. I couldn't wait.

"Well, then let's go," I said happily.

"Where?" Jack lowered his brows at me.

"To Longrigg Wood. There are jumps all over the place and that huge stretch of open grassland in the middle."

"That's one of the places where Solace ran away with me," said Mary, biting her lip, and the black horse started jogging and dancing around nervously.

"See that?" Jack asked her sternly. "You tensed up, tightened your fingers, stiffened your body, and that's the result. Solace needs to know you're relaxed and confident. That's why he does so well for you in the ring."

Mary made a visible effort to relax, only to squeal with alarm when Maggie, who'd been sitting quietly at the edge of the ring, suddenly ran back towards the stables, barking furiously.

"Calm down," Jack told Mary, who looked completely frightened. "Solace isn't bothered by your dog at all, it's your reaction that makes him prance around like that."

"Sorry…" Mary was fighting to hold back tears so I said quickly, "What's made Maggie so mad anyway? Should we take a look?"

We rode back through the archway leading to the stables. Maggie was standing just inside the yard, her neck outstretched as she continued to bark her warning. We saw immediately what she'd been trying to tell us – there, lounging insolently against a stable door was the tall, bulky figure of Kyle Pritchard.

Chapter Three

Kyle's face was a real picture when he saw Jack and I. His usual nasty sneer had been replaced by what he probably thought was an engaging smile.

"Jack, Billie! Nice to find you here!"

"Why's that, Kyle?" Jack rode Cody right up close to him. "You've never been happy to see us before."

"Oh, come on. Just because we've been rivals at a few cross country events doesn't mean we can't be friends."

"The reason we're not friends has nothing to do with competing against each other." Jack turned pointedly back to Mary. "Are you happy to have this person in your stable yard, Mary?"

"No, I'm not." She was pale but she urged Solace forward bravely. "What do you think you're doing here, Kyle?"

"Didn't Paul tell you?" His heavy face tried to register innocent surprise. "He said we could come in anytime to take measurements." As he spoke, a shortish, bow-legged man appeared from inside one of the storerooms.

I recognized his weaselly features – this was the new groom.

"Measurements for what?" I brought Gem alongside the other two horses, and we sat glaring down at Kyle who was still leaning against the door.

"For the alterations and improvements we'll make when my dad buys this place. We'll probably tear down most of this and put in something more up-to-date and streamlined."

"You can't do that!" Mary gasped. "It would break Paul's heart."

Kyle shrugged and said, "Not my problem," and tried to move away from us, but Jack and Cody barred his way.

"This is just another way of tormenting Mary, isn't it?" Jack looked pretty dangerous, I thought, all lean and mean and angry.

"What's it to you?" Kyle had abandoned his pretense that we were friends. "She's just a little wimp from England. Paul was more or less ready to sell before she came along."

"I don't know what you're talking about," said Jack, reining Cody back in disgust. "And I don't care. There's no excuse in the world for scaring her horse into bolting. You've always been pretty mean Kyle, but you've gone too far this time."

Kyle tried to step away from us, but I deliberately moved Gem forward at the same time and was delighted when my pony stepped heavily on his foot.

"Ow!" He hopped around in what I hoped was agony. "You did that on purpose, you little black-haired witch."

He reached up and for a scary moment I thought he was going to pull me off my horse but Jack was on him in a flash. "Take your hands off her! If you even touch Billie I'll break more than your riding whip."

I turned my head to look at him, just in time to see the weaselly man poked Cody hard in the ribs. Poor Cody shot forward, nearly knocking the still hopping Kyle to the ground.

"Eddie! You stupid idiot!" Kyle's face went a pasty white as he glared at his groom. "Get these silly kids away from me."

Eddie grabbed at Cody and tried to shove him back hard. Jack was ready for him and turned the bay pony swiftly, backing him up until he'd pinned the man against the wall.

"If either of you lays a hand on my girlfriend or my horse again you'll be sorry." I had never heard Jack sound so furious. And I'd never heard him call me his girlfriend before either. In spite of the tense situation I felt a nice warm glow.

"Leave them alone, Jack, they're not worth bothering with." Mary was looking a lot less nervous now. "They can shove off and not come back."

"We're going, we're going…" Kyle gave his sore foot one last rub and limped cautiously past Solace. "Come on, Eddie. I'll take this up with Paul later."

"Forget it." Mary sounded very commanding. "I'll make sure Paul doesn't allow you into Longrigg again."

"Fine." The look he gave her was pure evil. "I can wait until my dad's the owner. I'll have fun watching you leave this place, you little English sissyface."

We watched them climb into a shiny, pretentious-looking SUV and peel out of the yard.

"Phew!" Mary wiped her brow. "That felt so good. You two were fantastic – I've been really frightened of Kyle but today he looked more pathetic than terrifying."

"It's the same with most bullies," Jack said. "They're only tough when the odds are in their favor. It's been easy for Kyle, picking on you. He's twice your size, and he's got that creepy groom to back him up."

"Eddie! Of course!" With the light of battle in her eyes I thought Mary looked like anything but a sissy. "That's how Kyle nearly always manages to arrive in Longrigg Woods just after I do," she continued. "I have to ride past his house to get to the woods and that – that Eddie is usually hanging about when I do. I expect he's been told to report to Kyle whenever he sees Solace and me."

"I'm sure you're right," I chuckled. "Didn't Gem do a good job of squashing Kyle's foot? And the groom's face when Cody pinned him against the wall!"

"I enjoyed it," Mary said frankly. "I just hope they don't start giving you trouble because you're backing me up, Billie."

"I'll be OK," I said easily. "Jack's always with me when I ride and, even though Kyle is older and heavier, he's still scared to death."

"I'm not surprised," Mary laughed. "The way Jack leaped to your defense was enough to frighten anyone off. And of course there was the time he really did break a stick over Kyle's head, wasn't there?"

"Yeah, and that day I reported him to the show organizers for mistreating the horses too. There were also another couple of incidents when I've had to teach Kyle a lesson. I can't stand seeing him thrash his horses."

"I just can't stand seeing him, period," I said, and we all laughed.

"Would you like to come inside and meet my cousin Paul?" Mary asked. "We deserve a drink, and I can make sure Paul knows he must keep Kyle and Eddie out of Longrigg."

"OK." I was itching to see the house and longing to find

out what Kyle meant about buying Longrigg. "Can we put Gem and Cody in one of the empty stables?"

"Sure," Mary said. "Come on. Oh, Maggie I haven't told you what a good girl you were for letting us know those two creeps were around."

Maggie wagged her fluffy tail happily and trotted at Mary's side as we walked over to the back door of the big house. We took off our boots on the porch and padded into a big, warm kitchen. It was nice, all bright and sunny with pine cupboards and sparkling tiles. I think I'd been expecting something dark and gothic with an ancient stove and cobwebs hanging from the ceiling.

"I like your house," I said to Mary as she got three cans from the fridge.

"Mm. Paul's done wonders already, I think. He's got the heating sorted out, and renovated our rooms and the bathrooms, and his studio of course."

"Oh yeah, you said he was a painter. Can we see any of his stuff?"

Jack gave me a nudge. "Don't be so pushy Billie. Paul probably won't appreciate us nosing around."

"He'll be fine," Mary laughed. "Come and say hello."

We followed her out into a huge, high-ceilinged hallway. Now this was more like it, I thought, gazing around at the somber paneling and gray flagstones.

"This is where we watch TV." Mary pushed open a door to a big, comfortable room. "Paul calls it the drawing room, very English of him. And here's the dining room," she said, showing us into another massive, lofty place with heavy furniture that looked old.

"It's so clean." I was surprised. "Who does that? Not your cousin?"

29

"No, Paul has a housekeeper. She's nice too and a great cook."

"Should we just go to the studio so you can tell Paul about Kyle?" Jack wasn't comfortable with being shown around, but I couldn't get enough of it.

"We're on our way." Mary stopped at the foot of a curving staircase. "It's up two flights of stairs, I'm afraid."

"Great!" I was inspecting one of the rather somber paintings on the paneled walls. "This one isn't by Paul, is it?"

Mary laughed again. She was getting better at it. "No, it's a portrait of one of our ancestors. He looks a bit fierce, doesn't he?"

"They all do." I was looking at several other paintings where men and women in old-fashioned clothes looked sternly out at us. "Oh maybe not – here's a nice, smiley lady and look, she's got Maggie with her!" The portrait was of a dark-haired woman wearing a formal velvet ball gown and at her feet, gazing up adoringly, was a cream-and-gray bundle of shaggy hair.

"Well spotted, Billie," Mary said approvingly. "She's my great-aunt, Paul's mother, but that isn't Maggie in the portrait, it's one of her predecessors. I think she was called Beryl or she might have been Sukey, Peta, or Betsy. I could actually show you them all, though I don't suppose you want –"

"Sure we do!" I was fascinated. I'd never been in a house like this in my life. Jack looked less convinced but he followed us back down the hall.

"This is one of the rooms Paul hasn't got round to yet." Mary hesitated outside a heavy oak door. "I'd better warn you it's a bit gruesome if you're animal lovers."

"Why?" I was intrigued and held my breath when she opened the door. The room was very dark, with shuttered

windows keeping out the sun. It was smaller than the others we'd peeped at and the air smelled stale and stuffy.

"Sorry…" Mary was feeling around the door frame. "I can't find the light switch. Oh, there we are."

The room was flooded with light, and Jack and I both gave an involuntary gasp and took a step back. The walls were paneled like the hall but here there were animal heads, stags and lions and tigers, their majestic faces looking sightlessly through glass eyes as they hung against the oak walls.

"Oh yuck, gross!" I was aghast. "Did Paul's father kill all those beautiful animals?"

"No, they've been here for years apparently." Mary was moving across the floor. "In the old days people liked to hunt and shoot, then get their trophies stuffed and mounted. I don't think my great uncle was responsible for any of the heads but he could have been, he was pretty arrogant by all accounts. His eccentricity is demonstrated by something else."

"Oh no, what?" I felt very nervous, as if Mary was going to show us a collection of Egyptian mummies or something.

"These were all out on display when I got here." She opened a cupboard. "But I thought they were so awful I made Paul put them away."

She stood back, and Jack and I peered into the tall cupboard. I jumped and clenched my hands in fright. I was holding onto Jack's arm at the time, and I pinched him really hard.

"Ow!" He took my hand comfortingly. "It's OK, Billie. They're all stuffed too, aren't they Mary?"

"Mm-hm," she said, looking at the weird, ghostly shapes

32

of the four Tibetan Terriers on the shelves. "Paul said his father adored the dogs, especially the one who followed his wife around all the time, the lady in the portrait you saw. So when Sukey, Beryl, Peta, and Betsy died he had them stuffed and put on display in here. All the heads are bad enough but I think these are really horrible, don't you?"

"Yuck." I just wanted to leave. "Really gross. I hope you haven't shown them to Maggie."

"She's never shown the slightest interest in them." To my relief Mary shut the cupboard door, and we hurried out of the musty room and back to the staircase.

I felt very shaky and couldn't even admire Mary's pretty bedroom, which had its own luxury bathroom.

"I think there are 14 bedrooms," she said, "but they're not all refurbished yet, so I won't show you them all. We go through this door now and up the next lot of stairs to reach Paul."

The second staircase was much more narrow and plain than the first. Jack said it would have originally led to the servants' rooms.

"That's right." Mary and Maggie were leading the way. "Paul's made a lovely self-contained flat downstairs for his housekeeper and her husband, and all the rooms up here have been knocked into one for his studio. Here we are."

She knocked briskly on the door and we stepped from the old house into what looked like another world.

Chapter Four

It was dazzlingly bright to begin with. After the spooky darkness of the trophy room and the dim, narrow stairway this room seemed bursting with light and space. By knocking down walls Paul had transformed the original small rooms into one huge airy studio. Its white walls and pale, silver-gray floorboards reflected the light that flooded through dozens of gabled windows. The other thing that stunned you was the color. The studio was full of color, in the paintings and sketches on the walls, in the palette and easel set up to catch a soft westerly light, and in the clothes of the man who stood before it. He was wearing a bright orange shirt and dark green pants, both of which were daubed all over in blobs of red, blue and yellow.

"Hi Paul," Mary greeted him warmly. "Here's Billie and Jack to meet you."

Paul put down the paintbrush immediately and limped forward, his hand outstretched.

"Delighted to meet you. I'm so glad Mary has found some friends. It must be lonely for her here."

"I told you I like it here," Mary said firmly. "But it is nice to have these two around. They're going to help me with my riding."

"Well, you look fine to me, but of course I haven't been able to ride out with you." He looked worried again.

"Paul hurt his leg a month or two back," Mary explained. "He's had to stop riding while it heals."

"I've watched Mary in the ring," Paul said as he turned his gentle blue eyes towards us. "And she was wonderful but, of course, neither she nor Solace are used to the open countryside. I've been concerned for her going out alone although she doesn't complain."

"Well, don't worry," I said. I thought he was really nice. "Jack and I will go with her from now on. I take it Mary hasn't told you about Kyle Pritchard?"

I was all ready to tell him about the hassle Mary had been getting but she butted in quickly, "Kyle was here Paul, in the stable yard with his groom. He said you told him he could take some measurements."

"Hmm, I might have," Paul replied vaguely.

"Oh Paul, you mustn't sell Longrigg." Mary looked close to tears at the thought. "Tell him, Billie, tell him he can't let our family's house go!"

I felt a bit embarrassed at suddenly being involved, so instead I asked, "Is there – um – a reason you want to leave?"

"Well." He sat down on a scarlet sofa and beckoned us to do the same. "I thought I was doing OK. I'm slowly making the house comfortable again after it's been neglected for so long, but it's taken most of the money my father left. My original idea was to use all these wonderful rooms as a sort of a residential artists' summer school for other painters, sculptors, potters, you know the kind of

36

thing. Then, well the money situation became critical. I had a bad fall and broke my leg and, to top it off, the news from England was bad, and my lawyers weren't sure whether Mary would be allowed to come over here."

"It's all my fault, isn't it?" Mary's voice was sad, and I felt so sorry for her. "If you hadn't had to spend so much sorting out my guardianship –"

"Mary, I wanted you here," Paul said firmly. "I promised myself when your mother died that there would always be a home for you. Though whether that home will be Longrigg –"

"So Kyle's father stepped in with an offer, did he?" I could just imagine Kyle's family lording it over everyone in town if they moved into this big house.

"Yes. I met him one day when I was feeling particularly low, and he came up with a price that was very generous."

"He can afford it, no problem, but he'll ruin the house," I said scornfully. "Kyle's already talking about knocking things down."

"No!" Paul looked shocked. "I've been very careful to keep the exterior looking exactly the same as when my family started living here 250 years ago."

"So just tell Pritchard you've changed your mind," I said. "You haven't signed anything."

"I know," he sighed and ran his hand through his long hair. "But the problem about the money hasn't changed."

"And like I said, that's my fault." Mary was obviously feeling the pain of guilt. "My parents didn't appoint a guardian, you see Billie, and the lawyers handling their estate were going to make the English court responsible for me. Paul is my only living relative, and we've always been very fond of each other. He spent a fortune getting his

37

lawyers to grant guardianship to him. If he hadn't done that he wouldn't have to even think about Pritchard's offer."

"It was worth every penny to get you here," Paul smiled fondly at her. Although he was tall and dark and she was blonde and small, they looked alike, I thought, with their light blue eyes and the same slightly timid manner. "Anyway, who knows, the fabled Longrigg Emerald might just turn up and solve all our problems!"

"The Longrigg Emerald!" I looked at Mary. "What's that about?"

"Oh Paul's teasing me because he knows I spend half my time searching for the thing." She blushed slightly but raised her head defiantly. "He says he's never really believed in it, but I do."

"I think Mary's gotten carried away with the romantic idea of a hidden treasure," Paul said indulgently. "My father was a well-known eccentric but I can't believe even he would have squirreled away something so valuable."

"It was your father who hid it?" Jack was fascinated by stories about the old man whose bad temper and weird ways had been the talk of our town when we were both little.

Paul nodded. "So he said. He definitely bought a fabulous emerald to have made into a necklace for my mother, but she died suddenly before he'd had it done. I was very young but I remember how distraught he was when she died. He'd always been, well – different from other people I guess you'd say – but after her death he went right off the deep end."

"That must have been awful for you." I thought of the terrible life he must have led.

"I didn't see much of him, sad to say. He sent me away

to boarding school and we never got to know each other, and then after college I spent most of my time in Italy, learning about art. It puzzled my father that I'd rather paint wildlife than shoot it. He didn't understand the artist in me at all. But he was fond of me in his own way."

"So why did he hide the emerald from you?" I asked bluntly. It didn't sound too fond to me.

"Like I said, I'm not convinced he did. He did once tell me with great glee that he'd put it somewhere obvious if I used my brain to find it. He would tell me, 'The clue's in the name,' but I had no idea what he meant."

"But that was years ago," Mary protested. "You must have tried to figure it out and find the emerald before now."

"Well yes, I admit I looked everywhere I could think of," he said defensively. "But I was never able to come up with anything clever, and he never did get around to explaining what he meant. To be honest, I thought if he had hidden it somewhere it would've turned up during the renovations on the house. There was no urgency, not until now."

"Maybe he sold it," suggested Jack, always the practical one.

"Maybe he did," Paul agreed readily. "I mean, there are secret panels and hiding places, all the things you'd expect in an old house like this, but I think I know them all and the emerald's not in any of them."

"Well!" I felt very excited. "So now we've got two projects, Jack. Help Mary get ready for that Hunter Trial and find the missing emerald."

Jack gave me another of his dirty looks. "Yes, well, we'd better get started on the riding. Shall we take the horses to Longrigg Woods, Mary?"

"OK," she said, a little reluctantly I thought.

She asked Paul to look after Maggie as we were going out, and made him promise to keep Kyle out of the grounds in future. We then trooped back down the two staircases and outside.

"Phew!" I said as I tugged on my boots. "It's like the plot of a fantastic movie. Missing emeralds and sinister bad guys!"

"Let's just concentrate on the riding problem," said Jack and led the way back to the stables.

We rode along the drive and turned towards Longrigg Woods.

"Kyle's house is just along here," Mary said, already looking nervous.

"Relax," Jack told her. "You're tensing up and making Solace jog again. There's nothing to worry about."

We passed the big house that belonged to Kyle's father and I peered nosily over the hedge. It was big, with beautiful gardens, but I thought it couldn't compare to Longrigg and said so to Mary.

Her face lit up immediately. "Longrigg is really special, isn't it? I already love it almost as much as Paul does."

"I can't believe he'll sell it," I said. I was fascinated by the subject but Jack clearly wasn't. "Come on, you two," he said impatiently. "Let's get these horses warmed up with a working trot."

We moved briskly along the lane, and I decided not to tell Mary I was sure there'd been a weaselly face watching us from one of the Pritchards' windows. We soon reached the edge of Longrigg Woods. It's not my favorite ride (I like the open space of the hills better) but it has nice soft, leaf-covered trails in dappled shade that curve and twist between beech, oak, and hazel trees. There are jumps everywhere. Most of the riders who visit the woods like to build obstacles using fallen tree trunks or broken branches, and some of them are very solid and sturdy. Jack was still leading the way, obviously in charge, with Mary following and me bringing up the rear so I could keep an eye on her. We reached a narrow trail that had been turned into a jumping lane with several homemade fences rigged up between the two lines of trees. Jack turned round to check we were ready, then put Cody into a collected canter and started jumping his way along the lane. Mary followed, looking good, and I was impressed with the way Solace dealt with each jump, snapping his front legs back and clearing each one with style. Jack pulled up a short way beyond the last jump and asked her how it had gone.

"Fine." She was looking a lot less nervous. "It's easy following you and Cody. Solace isn't doing his usual pulling like a train and rushing-at-everything trick."

"That's because you're relaxed and comfortable, and that makes him feel the same. We'll do a few more like this and then I want to watch you take Solace over something on his own."

"OK," she agreed obediently, and we set off again.

We cleared a big log pile, a stile, several ditches, and a stream and were now approaching the stretch of open grassland where Mary had been run away with.

"Stay behind me across here and don't let Solace try and race Cody. He might try, it's a natural reaction when horses gallop together, but I want you to control his pace."

Mary nodded, looking pale but determined. She was actually doing really well, keeping her horse's black nose well away from Cody while sitting quietly and perfectly

41

balanced, when from the clump of trees behind us came an enormous "bang!" and then the crashing and flapping of wings as a flock of wood pigeons were frightened into the air. Even the normally bomb-proof Gem was startled into putting in a dramatic sideways shy, nearly shifting me out of the saddle. The more highly strung Solace was clearly terrified and reacted the only way he knew: by bolting headlong across the grass, galloping mindlessly in his effort to get as far away as he could from the petrifying noise.

Chapter Five

Although Mary gave her usual squeal of fright, she didn't panic the way she had in the hills. She kept her head and remembered to give and take with one rein, talking soothingly to the frightened horse until he dropped his head and began cantering in the wide circle she was using to calm him.

"Good stuff, Mary." I joined her as she brought Solace to a slightly shuddering halt. "What on earth was that? It sounded like a gun, only louder."

"It was a firecracker." Jack came thundering up to us, looking grim. "I went back to catch who threw it but they'd already got away. Not that I needed to see their faces to know who it was."

"Kyle and his groom?" I raised my hands in despair. "What chance have we got if they're going to resort to dirty tricks like that? We can't prove it was them and they can do it any time they like."

"I'd love to have another little word with Kyle." Jack clenched his fist expressively. "But like you said, it won't do any good – with their "lookout system", they're going to know every time we come to this place and they'll follow along with their firecrackers and whatever else they've got to scare us with."

"So let's find somewhere else." Mary was still white and very shaky.

"It's difficult," I said. "There are great rides around here but this is the only place that kind of mirrors a cross-country course. Unless..."

"Unless what?" she looked at me hopefully.

"Well, I was going to suggest you ask Paul if there was anywhere inside Longrigg's grounds that would do? We need a stretch of open country to get Solace used to galloping and a few jumps – we could build those, couldn't we Jack?"

He was frowning at me again. "You can't turn Longrigg into an event course," he said crossly. "Anyway, why should we hide away from Kyle Pritchard?"

"We won't be," I argued. "We'll only be working with Mary's practice. It'll drive him wild not being able to ruin things for her."

"I think it's a great idea," Mary said. "There's a fairly wild part of the grounds over on the northern side. There used to be a fishing lake and there's a thicket of trees and a long, winding turf trail."

"It sounds perfect," I said cheerfully, ignoring the black look Jack was giving me. "You ask Paul and let me know. If he agrees we can come over in the morning and figure out a course for you."

"Thanks Billie, you're really good to me."

I thought she looked about to cry again, so I quickly headed Gem towards the trail that led home. We escorted

Mary to her gate and watched until she and Solace disappeared from view.

"Honestly!" Jack glared at me. "Look what you've done now!"

"What?" I said innocently, thinking how good-looking he was even when he was mad.

"Now we're doing even more with this emotional girl and her problems."

"Mary's getting tougher by the minute," I protested. "I thought she dealt with the firecracker pretty well."·

"She still squealed and made a fuss. You didn't even mention that Gem nearly threw you off."

"Oh, that's ridiculous," I said. "Anyway, we've got to help her. We promised we would."

He was still scowling, "I don't see why."

"Because, aside from Paul, we're all she's got, that's why. No wonder that cousin of hers welcomed us with open arms."

"He's another one." Jack was determined to be gloomy. "The first time we meet him and he tells us all that stuff about a missing emerald! They're both weird."

"Look, just because their lives and their house are a lot different from ours doesn't make them weird. I think it's exciting, the thought of hunting for the missing jewel and building our own cross-country course."

"I don't mind that part," he admitted, "even though it still feels like chickening out from meeting Kyle. But I'm not getting involved with any emerald."

"Why not?" I was annoyed at his attitude.

"Because…" he hesitated a moment, looking unexpectedly shy. "I don't want to spend all our time with other people. I like it best when it's just you and me."

47

I was secretly thrilled and thought he looked gorgeous with that soft, vulnerable expression on his face. I had to shake myself to get back to reality. "We can't dump Mary. Think of what she's been through and the hell Kyle is giving her now."

He grunted a slightly reluctant agreement. "OK, I'll try to find out just why he's doing it. Kyle's always been a pain, and I can see why he's eager for his father to buy Longrigg, but there must be more to it than that. He really seems to hate Mary so I suppose you're right about not ditching her. I'm with Paul though, I really can't believe in this crazy idea of a hidden emerald – you girls can waste your time with that!"

We rode back to the yard and did all our chores, then spent the rest of the day listening to some CDs my oldest brother had given me. I had to admit Jack was right. It really was great when we were alone. I kept thinking about how Jack had told Kyle I was his girlfriend and reliving the wonderful way it had made me feel. I came back to earth when Mary phoned and told me Paul had agreed we could use the far end of the grounds for her riding practice.

"I don't think he was very keen at first," she said. "And of course I didn't want to make a big deal about the way Kyle's been behaving."

"I don't see why not." I'd said as much to Jack earlier. "Paul should know what Kyle's been up to. He'd be furious that you've been harassed like that and it might make him refuse to sell Longrigg to the Pritchards."

"But I can't put that kind of pressure on him," she explained, a little forlornly. "You know I feel responsible for him even having to consider selling. Because of me, Paul can't afford his dream of making Longrigg pay as an artists' summer school. If we could find the missing emerald, Billie, it would be like all our dreams come true."

She could use a few dreams coming true in her life, I thought, and didn't tell her Jack was reluctant to help solve the mystery of the emerald.

"I'll start racking my brains," I promised. "See you in the morning."

It was all very well telling her that, I thought as I drifted into sleep. The idea of finding a missing anything in a house the size of Longrigg was daunting enough but without any real clue to help us I just didn't know where to start.

Jack was on our doorstep bright and early the next morning and gave his usual heart-stopping grin when he saw me. We pedaled off to the yard and were soon riding the ponies towards Longrigg House. This time Mary wasn't waiting for us, but we could hear excited barking so we knew Maggie was around somewhere. We found the little dog jumping up at the door of a garden shed.

"Hi Mary, are you in there?" I called and she poked her head out and said hello.

"I'm trying to find any tools that might help with the jump building," she said. "Do we need nails and stuff?"

"No, we're not putting up anything permanent, just enough different obstacles for you to practice with during the next couple of weeks," Jack said. "Let's get going."

We rode sedately through the rose garden that bordered Longrigg's towering walls, accompanied by an ecstatic Maggie who pranced happily around Solace's feet.

"She's thrilled because I've let her join in today." Mary smiled down at the little dog. "Paul says she pines the whole time when I shut her in the house, so as we're not leaving the grounds this morning I thought it would be OK."

49

"I love the way she follows you," I said, bringing Gem in behind Solace as Mary trotted across a rougher stretch of grass leading uphill to a wooded area. Jack and I were excited at what we saw when we reached the top. The little thicket was perfect for building log piles, and there was already a solid-looking stile and a gate we could jump, plus plenty of hefty fallen branches to use. The wood dropped away to the long gallop Mary had described on one side and, on the other, to our delight, was a good-sized lake, nice and shallow at the edges and deep in the middle.

"I'd like to build something very inviting at the edge of the water," Jack said. "Billie can tell you that you'll definitely get a jump like that in a cross-country event."

"Always," I agreed. "They usually have a straightforward fence which you jump normally, but you land in the water, take a few strides to the other side, and sometimes there's another jump there too, which takes you back onto dry land. You don't want to get it wrong – if you do you'll end up very wet!"

"I don't think Solace has ever done a jump like that." Mary looked worried. "We've met a water jump in the show-jumping ring but you have to clear that completely, you get penalized if your horse drops even one foot in it."

"That's right, but in cross country Solace will have to learn to get his feet wet," Jack said. "It shouldn't be a problem, though. Most horses are happy to do it."

We spent the whole morning dragging planks and branches around, and riding our ponies over the fences we built to test if they were OK. It was hard work but fun, and Mary began to look a lot happier again. She was still more confident if she and Solace could follow Gem or Cody over the various jumps but she tried hard to build up the courage to take him through the course on her own. Aside from one or two girlish squeaks when Solace took a jump too fast, she did really well. The only fence she had no success at all with was at the lake. Solace would not and did not go anywhere near that water. We tried putting him close behind Cody, but as soon as the black horse saw the gleam of water he put on all the brakes and refused point blank to go any further. We tried Cody in front of him, Gem close behind – no good. We tried going in tandem, Solace cantering neck-and-neck with Gem, but when my dappled guy rose easily in the air to splash merrily in the lake, Solace ducked sideways and just kept cantering in a curving line around the edge of the water.

"He just won't put his toes in the wet stuff," Jack said, exasperated. "I suppose it's a completely foreign thing for him to do. He's always been told to jump clear over water before."

"Hasn't he ever enjoyed a paddle at the beach?" I asked, thinking about all the fun Mary and Solace had missed.

"Oh well, let's end on a good note," Jack said. "Put him over that stile, Mary, and make sure he clears it well. Plenty of impulsion, but don't try and override him into the fence, just relax and let him keep his balance and his pace, and he'll be happy to soar over it."

Mary calmed her horse, who'd been getting pretty fed up with her attempts to get him in the water. As soon as they turned away from the lake, he stopped fighting and softened into a perfect outline. Mary popped him over the stile, cantering easily on landing. She brought him to a halt so she could get off and pick Maggie up. The little dog still looked happy but very tired. She hadn't stopped running around all morning, and she settled immediately in her place in front of Mary on the saddle. They made a pretty picture, the gleaming black horse, his petite blonde rider, and the attractive little dog, her sparkling collar glinting through her shaggy hair. We cooled down by walking back to the yard, where Mary dismounted and put Maggie back on the ground.

"You're a good little Tibetan Terrier," she told the dog fondly and grinned at us. "Want a drink and a sandwich? You can turn Cody and Gem out for a munch in one of the smaller paddocks if you like."

I could see Jack was going to say no, so I said quickly, "That'd be great!" and we did what she suggested.

The kitchen was very clean and quiet and Mary explained the housekeeper had gone shopping.

"There's plenty of cheese though," she said as she opened the fridge. "And help yourselves to a can of something."

As soon as we'd finished eating Jack was on his feet, ready to go home.

"Hang on," I said. "I wanted another look around, to maybe try and work out if there are any more clues about the missing emerald."

"Paul said he's looked." Jack was sulky. "So what chance do *we* have?"

"None if we don't try. Come on Mary, show us around again."

She led the way through what seemed a bewildering number of rooms. The ones Paul hadn't refurbished were the worst to hunt in, all dark and spooky with heavy oil paintings in ornate frames.

"Who are all these people?" I pointed to yet another ancient man in nineteenth-century clothes.

"I can't name them all, though Paul can of course," Mary

said, peering around the room. "I know which one is Paul's father, there he is, look."

We stared at the portrait of a man who was a heavier, sadder version of Paul.

"Here's another one of him, riding his favorite horse." Mary had moved further along. "Paul named one of his own mares after this one. She was called Jewel."

"Really?" I walked over to take a look, then did a double-take. "Jewel! Paul's father called his horse Jewel. It's a clue to the emerald, it must be! We've found our first clue!"

Chapter Six

To say the other two were less than impressed is putting it mildly.

"How can it be a clue?" Jack said irritably. "It's just a name. He could have had a horse called anything."

"But he didn't – the mare's name was Jewel and that's what Paul's father meant by telling Paul he'd find the emerald if he used his brains. I'm using mine and I think Jewel equals Emerald."

"You could be right," said Mary, concentrating hard. "But where does that take us? If the horse is the clue, where is the emerald?"

"Well, I don't know exactly," I said, peering closely at the painting. "Maybe it's hidden in a panel behind this picture."

"I've seen movies where the safe is hidden behind a big portrait." I was pleased to see Jack trying to show an interest. "Can we take this one off the wall, Mary?"

"Sure." She clambered onto a chair and tried to lift the heavy frame. "You'll have to help me, Jack."

Jack is very tall and strong but even he buckled a little at the weight of the painting. They rested it carefully against a sofa, and we spent ages going over every panel in the wall. There were a lot of cobwebs and one enormous spider which made Mary squeak when it nearly ran across her arm. I'm not wild about creepy crawlies myself but years of being teased by big brothers meant that I hardly flinched and was rewarded when Jack put his arm round me in a brief hug.

"I don't think there's anything here, Billie." He stopped tapping at the panels. "It was a good idea but obviously not the right answer."

"The horse named Jewel could still be the clue," I argued. "There might be other paintings or photographs of her around the house."

"There probably are," Mary agreed. "My family seems to have been very keen on having their portraits painted and a lot of them include the animals they owned."

The way she said "my family" in a shy but proud way made me feel all emotional. I often moan about my big, boisterous family but I'd hate to be without them. I couldn't imagine how Mary must feel now that she only had one cousin and a houseful of paintings to relate to. I really wanted to help her find this missing emerald so she and Paul could carry on living in the family home that meant so much to them. The trouble was, I couldn't for the life of me think of anywhere else to look.

"We ought to go." Jack was itching to get away.

"I want to help Mary search some more," I said.

"You go on back to the yard if you like."

"But I can't leave you here, can I?" he said crossly, and I stared at him.

"Why not?"

"Because Kyle might be hanging around when you leave. He's nasty enough to bear a grudge about you getting Gem to stand on his foot."

"So you're going to be my bodyguard?" I loved the idea but I couldn't say so, could I? "Oooh, my hero!"

He went red and shuffled his feet in an embarrassed way so I took pity on him.

"OK. I'd rather not meet Creepy Kyle and Weasel Eddie on my own. We'll come by tomorrow for more practice, Mary. Maybe you can have a good look to see if there's anything else in the house that has to do with Jewel."

"I'll ask Paul. He knows where everything is and a lot of old stuff from the rooms has been stored in the cellars. I haven't even been down there yet."

Some of the rooms in the main house, especially that horrible trophy one, were spooky enough, I thought, without having to creep around in a dark and gloomy underground cellar. We went back outside and collected our happy-looking ponies from the lush paddock where they'd spent their lunch time. Jack was happy too, now that we were leaving. He rode Cody on the outside of Gem all the way, twisting in the saddle every so often to make sure we weren't being followed.

"Kyle and his groom are going to be furious when they realize Mary won't be riding past the Pritchard house any more." I laughed at the thought but Jack looked worried.

"I know, and I have the feeling they'll try something else. We'll have to keep watching them."

"We'll wear our brains out thinking about the missing emerald and wondering what Kyle's up to," I said lightly, but Jack's face darkened.

"Honestly Billie – I'm not crazy about poking around that house looking for something a loony old man probably threw out with the trash years ago."

"Oh, I'm sure he didn't!" I was adamant. "Paul says his father definitely bought an emerald, and I don't think he would have gotten rid of it. Besides being so valuable, it was a symbol of the love he felt for his wife. I think it's such a romantic story, him hiding the emerald away like that."

"And I think it's just stupid," Jack said grumpily. I thought it was time to change the subject.

"How did you think Mary did today? I thought she was good."

"Not bad," he said cautiously. "Except at the lake. Solace is being naughty about it, and she's got to be more determined, to really want to get him in that water. I think I might suggest I ride him tomorrow."

But to our surprise, the next day the seemingly docile Mary refused point blank to let Jack take Solace over the cross-country course.

"I've got to do it," she said. "I'm the one with the problem, and I've got to overcome it. I'm more determined than ever to enter that Hunter Trial and show Kyle I'm not such a coward."

"I know you're not a coward, it's just that I thought if I could get Solace to jump into the water once, he'd be more confident when you ask him."

"It might make him worse." Mary was beginning to show a really strong will. "Let me try again."

Although the rest of the practice went well, with Mary in complete control even on the fast gallop section, Solace still refused to have anything to do with the lake. For the next three days we tried every trick we could think of but with absolutely no success. It was a similar story with the emerald hunt. There were several other pictures of Jewel and one in particular, which also showed Paul's mother and her little Tibetan Terrier, gave us hope. We went over that picture inch by inch, looking for anything that might give us a further clue. Jack got more and more fed up with my insisting that we spend at least an hour every day searching for the missing jewel. After I'd finished crawling all over the painting yet again, he announced bluntly that he'd had enough and was going home. I was hot and irritable myself and snapped, "Fine, you go on. I'm staying here."

"I can't," he said, glaring at me. "What if Kyle –"

"Oh, I can take care of myself." I was exasperated at not finding anything and took my bad temper out on him. "Go away, Jack."

He gave me one last hurt look and stomped off without another word. I felt guilty but I wouldn't follow him even though I really wanted to. Instead I spent a horrible 45 minutes creeping nervously around the dark and dingy Longrigg's cellar. This was simply because we'd run out of places to look for "Jewel" clues in the house, and I had wondered if any of the old tack or stable fittings had been stowed away when Paul had spruced up the yard. I'm sure the cellar would have been very exciting to some people, but I hated it and so did Mary. Everything had been stacked neatly and the place was reasonably well lit, but there were sinister rustling noises and that grubby smell of old and damp.

One of the dust sheets draped over something fluttered. "What's that?" I turned to Mary.

"I think it's rats." She was even paler than usual. "Or maybe just mice. Oh help!"

I nearly jumped out of my skin and grabbed her hand quickly. "What's happened?"

"Sorry, it's only cobwebs. One of them wrapped itself around my face."

I picked off bits of cobweb out of her hair and tried to calm down.

"Paul said anything from the stables would be in the corner over there." She pointed. "Do we know what we're looking for, Billie?"

"No," I admitted, "but I thought if the name Jewel is the clue, maybe your great-uncle hid the emerald in something belonging to the horse rather than just a picture of it."

It didn't sound terribly convincing to me and I could see Mary wasn't enthusiastic about it either, but she nodded bravely and we started sifting through the pile of junk from the stable yard. It really was junk, leather reins so old they were as stiff as bone and crumbled at the touch. There were also rusted stirrup irons and buckles, ancient canvas rugs, and a box of weird-looking gadgets we could only guess at.

"I think this is a collar to stop a horse from wind sucking," I said, holding up a mildewed strap. "And these awful things are some kind of spurs."

"There's no way of telling which things belonged to which horse." Mary poked her finger tentatively in another box. "I mean, if they were labeled 'Dancer' and 'Cleo' and 'Jewel' it might be easier. Aaaaggggh!"

I clutched at her in fright, my shadow swooping eerily on the dingy brick wall.

"Mary, what is it?"

"A spider. No, lots of spiders. They all scuttled out of this box. Ugh, I hate this, I'm leaving."

"Me too. I'm sure there's nothing here, though maybe

61

we should see if there are any other pictures of Paul's father and Jewel."

"There aren't. At least Paul says there aren't and that's good enough for me."

Mary was moving rapidly back to the stone stairway, and I gladly followed her. We switched off the lights at the top of the stairs and bolted gratefully through the door and into the hallway.

"I feel as if spiders and mice are crawling all over me," Mary shuddered and picked frantically at the cobwebs still in her hair. "I'm going to have a shower, what about you?"

"Nah, I'll go home and have a bath." For once I couldn't get away quickly enough. "Then I'll go to Jack's and tell him he was right, it was a waste of time."

"He'll forgive you." Mary smiled at me. "You can't do anything wrong in his eyes."

I blushed a little but was happy she'd noticed. I brought Gem out of the field, nagging him gently because he'd obviously enjoyed a good roll, his usually sleek dappled flanks covered in dust and dirt.

"We make a wonderful pair, don't we?" I hugged him to show I wasn't really mad at him. "You're as mucky as I am. Let's hope no one sees us looking like this."

Mary had already disappeared to wash the cobwebs out of her hair so I set off down the drive, picking a few burrs out of Gem's mane as he walked. I honestly didn't give a thought to the possibility of Kyle or Eddie being around, since our yard lay in the opposite direction from the Pritchard house. As I turned Gem towards home my mind was full of the two problems we were facing, Solace's dislike of water and, of course, the mystery of the emerald. We seemed to have covered just about everything we could think of to do with Jewel, and I was trying to memorize all the rooms we'd seen, wondering if there'd been something we'd missed. Jack was concentrating on the Solace problem so it was up to me to produce a brainwave that would solve the missing jewel puzzle. I suppose it was because I was so deep in thought that I failed to notice a car that was nearly concealed in the trees opposite Longrigg's gates. I was vaguely aware of the sun glinting on its windshield but too absorbed to give it much thought. It was only when the engine started and the car slid out to drive slowly and menacingly behind me that I realized it was the same shiny SUV I'd seen once before. I turned sharply in the saddle. There was no mistake, in the passenger seat was Kyle, and the car, driven by the detestable Eddie, was heading straight for me!

Chapter Seven

It was traveling very slowly and, as it came alongside me, Kyle stuck his pudgy face out.

"If it isn't the little witch! And all on her own too. Where are your friends, Billie?"

"None of your business, Kyle." I stared back, determined to show I wasn't scared. Well I wasn't. Well, not very.

"So your little English friend is dropping out of the Hunter Trial?" he said with a nasty grin. "She'd better. She's such a chicken she'd only have fallen off and cried."

"There's nothing cowardly about Mary!" I retorted. "And you're wrong about her and the Hunter Trial. She'll be there. We all will."

"Well, you'd better take plenty of hankies to mop up her tears with, oh and another one for me to polish the cup I'm going to win." He really was a slimeball.

"Get lost, Kyle." I hated him. "There's always a bad smell when you're around."

He scowled then pointed to me and my pony and changed to a sarcastic laugh. "That smell is you and that

scruffy little rug rat you're riding." I'd forgotten how dirty Gem and I were but I shot back, "He was sharp enough the other day, wasn't he? How's your foot feeling, Kyle?"

He flushed a nasty brick-red color and began opening the door to get at me. As he did I saw, very clearly, the box of firecrackers that lay at his feet.

"So it was you, throwing firecrackers around to scare the horses," I said scornfully. "Well, you won't be able to use that dirty trick at the competition so I wouldn't bother clearing a space on your mantelpiece. We're going to take that trophy home, not you, you big cheating bully."

As he lunged forward to grab at me I touched Gem's sides and he responded at once, surging powerfully forward. It wasn't my fault that he gave Kyle a tremendous blow with his shoulder, pushing him off balance and sending him spinning to the ground. Kyle let out an enormous roar of pain and outrage, and I heard Eddie cursing freely as he stopped the car and leaped out. I didn't hang around, but just crouched low over Gem's neck and let him gallop practically flat out on the grassy shoulder of the lane. We rounded the corner and kept going until we reached the secluded bridle path that would take us back to the yard.

I slowed Gem down and patted him lovingly. "You were great. We showed 'em!"

We'd only walked a short way along the rutted trail when I heard the roar of an engine. Turning my head, I was horrified to see the SUV coming straight at me again, this time racing so fast it was jumping and jolting as it hit each ridge and pothole in the rough path. I couldn't see the expression on Kyle's face, but I thought it was safe to assume he wasn't too happy with me. I touched Gem's sides again

and my wonderful pony started cantering towards home and away from the SUV. It wasn't easy, since the bridle path is very rough and uneven and, although the car was getting thrown around behind us, I could hear it was gaining. Desperately I veered to the left, cantering Gem on the banked, tree-lined verge that edged the bridle path.

He had to swerve and bend his way through bushes and around trees, and it was only his great skill that kept us out of harm's way. The car was hurtling alongside us now and I could see Kyle's evil grin as he realized they'd soon be able to spin around in front of my pony and force us to stop. I urged Gem even faster and he flew across the narrow strip of ground. Twigs and branches lashed at my face and my hands were torn by brambles as we thundered desperately for the end of the trail and open ground. Then suddenly, wonderfully, I saw just ahead a tall figure on a dark bay pony, galloping straight towards the oncoming car. Jack! My heart leaped with joy. He kept riding until I was sure he'd have to either stop or veer out of the path of the oncoming SUV. I could see his face now, his dark eyes blazing as he and Cody came nearer and nearer.

Just as I was about to scream, "Jack, get out of the way, they'll run you down!" Eddie lost his nerve and swerved the car across the path, missing Jack by inches. I brought Gem to a halt and turned my scratched and bloodstained face towards my hero.

"Billie!" he spun Cody and raced over to me. "Are you all right? Did they hurt you?"

I raised my bleeding hands to my bleeding face. "I'm only scratched a little. Oh Jack –"

But before I could say a pretty thank-you speech, he'd turned his horse again with a roar of rage and was charging

towards the car. It accelerated immediately and jolted rapidly away in a great belch of exhaust fumes which left Jack coughing and furious. I called to him and he came back, his dark face grim. "I knew I never should have left you," he said as he reached out and touched my chin gently.

"I'm fine, honestly." I scrubbed hurriedly at the scratches to show him. "They didn't get me, these are just from the trees while we were trying to escape. It — it was great when I saw you riding to our rescue, Jack."

"I came back to find you but I guess I was a little late," he said, turning to look back to where the car had disappeared. "Were they waiting for you outside Longrigg? I passed the SUV on my way home and thought they were just going to the Pritchard house. When they saw me they must have realized you'd be around and on your own."

I nodded. "They were waiting outside the gate. And Jack — when Kyle opened the car door I saw he had firecrackers in there."

"Too bad they didn't give me a chance to see them," he said grimly. "We've got to report Kyle and that moron Eddie to somebody, Billie."

"You mean the police?" I asked and shook my head to say no. "Mary would be devastated if we did. She's trying to keep the trouble she's having with Kyle away from Paul. She has a theory that to tell her cousin would be putting pressure on him."

"What kind of pressure?" Jack said irritably. "Honestly, they make everything so complicated and hard on themselves."

"Mary won't say anything to persuade Paul not to sell to Pritchard because she says it's not fair, the money situation

isn't his fault, and she doesn't want to make him feel guilty."

"That sounds as clear as mud." Jack gave my hand a last squeeze and turned for home. "But I suppose it's what I've come to expect."

"Poor Mary." I felt very protective towards her. "She's trying really hard, you have to admit that."

"She's doing OK, I guess," Jack said. " But she's going to have to be more determined if she wants to overcome Solace's water phobia."

"We haven't got very long," I agreed. "And I don't know how much time we have to solve the emerald mystery."

"I can't think why you're bothering." Jack gave me a sidelong look. "But I don't want to fight with you again over it."

"Me neither. I'm sorry I got snippy with you earlier. You were right about it being a waste of time searching in the cellar. It was horrible too, really creepy."

"Oh well, now that you've done it you can give up the idea that the mystery is something to do with the horse being called Jewel. I think it's more important to stop Kyle and Eddie trying all these bully tactics on you two girls. You could have been badly hurt today, Billie."

"Well, I wasn't," I said cheerfully, feeling fine now that he was here. "And we've got to keep on trying to find the emerald. It's the only thing that will stop Kyle getting his own way."

He squared his shoulders and looked tough. "There are a few other things I'd rather do to stop him. Let's face it, there's absolutely no sense to this mystery – you're never going to solve it – never."

70

Chapter Eight

I felt very annoyed with him but I could hardly say so after he'd turned up like a knight in shining armor to rescue me. Instead, I changed the subject back to the safer one of Mary's riding practice. When we got back to the yard everyone was very concerned about my scratched and slightly battered appearance, but I passed it off by saying I'd tried out a new gallop trail which hadn't worked. I spent hours going over my brave Gem, finding only a few scratches but dabbing them gently with antiseptic anyway.

We were enjoing good weather so all the ponies were living out in the fields, which cut down on our stable chores. Jack and I sat on the gate and watched Gem and Cody trot over to join their friends. There was some gentle nose nuzzling and another comic display of rolling from Gem, which probably covered all my careful first aid with dust again, but he looked so happy I didn't complain.

"I wonder if they talk about their day like we do?" I asked Jack, and he grinned at me in that fabulous way of his.

"Probably not. But if they do, your Gem has an exciting

story to tell." He'd reluctantly agreed not to report Kyle and his groom, but he didn't waste any time in putting Mary in the picture the next day.

"I'm so sorry, Billie." Her small face looked mournful again. "I was worried Kyle might start on you next. Just what is it that makes him so mean?"

Jack had the answer. "For a start: he's been spoiled. His dad overcompensates for not spending any time with him by just buying him whatever he wants. I asked around about Eddie, oh don't worry Billie." Jack could see I was nervous. "I kept my promise and didn't report him for driving at you like that. They say he's a real bad guy, criminal record, the works. He's never going to get another real job so he plays up to Kyle and does any dirty work he's asked to do and probably enjoys it too. Kyle's definitely worse since Eddie arrived. Someone should tell Pritchard what a bad influence the guy is on his son. You really took on a lot, Mary, when you decided to stand up to Kyle."

"I'm glad I did," she said resolutely. "Even though he seems to be treating me worse than most."

"I think I know why that is," Jack said slowly. "Apparently Kyle's mother got fed up with being neglected too, and she ran off with a young English guy several years ago. Kyle's never forgiven her and puts a lot of the blame on the guy. When he found out you were from England, he unleashed a lot of the hatred he's been bottling up."

"That explains a lot but it doesn't excuse it." Mary was pale. "Well, I might be English but I'm not a coward. I'm going to get Solace to jump in that water, and I'm going to beat Kyle in that competition!"

We set off across the grounds with Maggie accompanying us as usual. The little dog ran happily at Mary's side, wagging

her tail joyfully until we reached the edge of the lake. We brought Gem, Cody, and Solace to a halt and waited while Jack thought up a strategy. Maggie sat at the black horse's hooves and looked up at us reproachfully.

"She doesn't like going in water either," Mary explained, smiling lovingly at the terrier. "If I ever manage to get Solace over that fence and into the lake it'll be interesting to see whether Maggie follows. My bet is she'll run round the outside and meet up with us when we come out."

"What a pair!" Jack said in exasperation. "Though I suppose it doesn't really matter whether Maggie goes in or not. It's different with Solace – you won't have a chance in the Hunter Trial if he ducks out at the water."

"I know, I know." Mary gritted her teeth. "I really want to do it, Jack. Any new ideas?"

"Well, he doesn't put the brakes on and stop," Jack said. "His usual way of avoiding the jump is to veer out to the left. If Billie and I stand at that side of the fence, holding Gem and Cody lengthways so we make a good long barrier, it should leave Solace nowhere to go but forward."

"And forward means over the jump and into the water," I added helpfully.

Mary groaned. "It sounds so easy, doesn't it? OK, let's give it a try."

Solace, nicely warmed up and with a few successful jumps already accomplished on the way, looked fit and eager and ready. Despite that, Mary's first two tries were hopeless with the black horse running out way before the approach to the lake.

"Toughen up, Mary," Jack called to her. "He's being silly, you've got to be determined and give him the confidence to go forward."

She nodded, her face pale but resolute. This time you could see the impulsion she used to drive Solace on, and Jack and I spread ourselves out at the side of the jump to prevent the black horse from ducking out. Everything looked good: Mary had him beautifully balanced and under control. Their pace was perfect, their approach positive. Solace seemed to roll his eyes towards us, as if weighing up the possibilities of making his usual escape on that side, then realizing he'd left it too late, thundered straight for the jump.

"He's going to do it!" Jack breathed, and I bobbed up and down with excitement. It seemed there was no way horse and rider could fail but, at the very last moment, instead of taking off in his soaring, athletic way, Solace slammed his hooves down, dropped his head, and sent poor Mary flying over his head and the fence, straight into the shallow water. Solace didn't gallop away, he just stood on dry land looking over the pile of logs to where Mary floundered and gasped in the lake. Maggie too, though clearly concerned at what her beloved owner was doing, made no attempt to join her, and Mary eventually hauled herself to her feet and squelched miserably out, looking very small and very, very wet.

"Oh thanks, Solace, thanks Maggie." She glared at them crossly. "So kind of you to stick with me. And thanks to you too, Jack!"

"Don't blame me." Jack was trying not to laugh. "It's not my fault, it was a perfectly good idea, and I still say if you were more determined Solace would just do it."

"We'll think of some other way," I said quickly, feeling sorry for Mary. "But not today. Let's get you back to the house and dried off."

"OK." She sounded very subdued, and we rode in silence until we'd almost reached the kitchen door.

"Oh no!" Mary pointed to where the familiar, hated SUV was parked at the side of the house. "Kyle must be here trying to get his measurements again."

"But he can't be." I looked at her in surprise. "I thought Paul was going to keep him out. And he's not parked by the stable yard so he and Eddie can't be snooping round there."

"He must be in the house then!" Mary was close to tears as she slid soggily to the ground and led Solace along the path.

I jumped off Gem and walked beside her. "Let me take your horse." I reached out for his reins. "I'll untack him while you go and change."

We'd nearly reached the back door, passing close to the Pritchards' SUV when Mary pointed tearfully to her dripping wet clothes. "I can't go indoors like this. Kyle might see me and he'll realize straight away I fell off in the lake. I can't let him know what a terrible time I'm having getting Solace to go into water. He and Eddie would probably soak us with a hose or push us in a stream next time we meet."

"You've got to go in the house and dry off." I tried to reason with her but she stood shivering, refusing to move.

"Look, I've got a really good idea for you and Solace tomorrow," Jack told her. "We'll forget the lake, you're both too wound up about it there. We'll try a nice, relaxing trip to the beach instead."

"Great idea!" I patted Mary's wet shoulder encouragingly. "We'll go there first thing tomorrow morning, have some fun, and get Solace to paddle his feet at the same time. He'll love it, I'm sure."

76

"OK." She looked very down, and I handed Solace and Gem's reins to Jack. "Jack will take the horses. You're coming indoors with me, Mary!"

She came meekly enough, and we went through the kitchen and up the first flight of stairs without seeing anyone. I ran a nice warm bath in her pretty coral-colored bathroom and left her to peel off the soggy clothes and climb in. As I opened the door I heard voices and slipped into Mary's bedroom to keep out of the way. I peeped through the half-closed door to see Paul, together with Kyle and an older man, walk past and start to go down the stairs. A few moments later Paul reappeared alone, his amiable face creased with worry.

"Paul!" I hissed. "Have they gone?"

He looked startled for a moment. "Oh, hello Billie. You mean the Pritchards? Yes, they've left."

"Good." I stepped out to join him. "I want to talk to you about them, well really about Kyle."

"He's an objectionable sort of kid, isn't he?" Paul ran a paint-splotched hand through his hair.

"I'll say," I hesitated, then made up my mind to go on. "Mary doesn't want me to tell you this, but Kyle's been giving her a terrible time. He and that groom of his have been trying to terrorize her into leaving here."

"What?" He sounded really shocked and I plunged on, filling in all the details of Kyle's nasty tricks.

"Good grief." Paul leaned against the wall as if he was too staggered to stay upright. "I can't believe Mary's been through all this. She hasn't said a word about it."

"She doesn't want to worry you," I said. "She thinks it's her fault that you're having to sell Longrigg."

"Do you mean because of the money?" Paul was grim-

faced. "It's true the legal costs in England were astronomical, but I wanted to bring Mary home. She was devastated by the death of her parents, and I think it's been worth every penny to get her here."

"She loves Longrigg too," I told him. "Despite everything Kyle has done she wants to stay here."

"You really think so?" he asked eagerly.

"Yes," I said. "She can't bear the thought of you selling the house, especially to a low-life like Kyle. Won't you reconsider your idea, Paul?"

"I'll have to." He straightened up and squared his shoulders. "I didn't think much of the Pritchards before you told me what Kyle had been doing, but the only other way of resolving my finances is to borrow heavily and I didn't want to do that. The bank will probably agree to a loan, but it will have to be secured on the house and my father would have detested the idea."

"Your father was — well — a little eccentric though, wasn't he?" I suddenly felt like I'd gone too far, but Paul didn't take offense.

"Oh yes, I know that. But I always felt I'd let him down already, going abroad the way I did and making my living as an artist. I didn't want to do something else he'd have hated, and I know for sure he felt that way about mortgaging Longrigg."

"He probably wouldn't have wanted an artists' school here either," I said candidly. "But it's what you want and, if it means you and Mary can stay here, then surely it's worth it."

"Of course it is." He gave me his tentative smile. "You're certainly very forthright and down to earth in your thinking, Billie. I'll bet it's a great relief to Mary having someone like you to talk to."

"She's pretty quiet actually. We mostly talk about our horses," I said and he looked worried again.

"She doesn't speak to you about her parents?"

I shook my head.

"She should, I think. Her mother was wonderful. Mary talks about her a lot to me."

"But you're family," I pointed out. "Maybe when she knows me better she'll take me into her confidence as well."

"True," he said. Like Mary he seemed almost pathetically pleased at the word "family". "In the meantime I suppose I should get on with the practical side of things. What do you think I should do first?" He wasn't like any other adult I knew, asking for advice from a 14-year-old in that way, but I guessed he just wasn't used to dealing with life's practicalities.

"Go and see the bank," I replied.

"You think so? I thought I'd call Pritchard up and tell him I'm not going to sell. The reason he and his thuggish son were here this morning was to put the pressure on. He told me I had to make up my mind one way or the other by this coming weekend. I've been stalling, trying to delay finally accepting his offer."

"Maybe you should make sure you can get a loan from the bank before you speak to Mr. Pritchard." I thought he probably needed that pointed out to him.

"Billie, you're right again. I'll wait until they give me a definite yes before I tell Pritchard he can keep his money and make sure his revolting son doesn't bother Mary again."

"Great." I smiled in relief.

We were still standing on the landing as Mary appeared at

her bedroom door, clean and dry again as she finished toweling her hair.

"What are you two doing?" She'd stopped crying and was doing her best to be cheerful. "I – um – decided to shower before lunch, Paul."

"It's OK," I told her, "Paul knows what happened this morning. I told him how you're trying to stand up against that bully Kyle and how you've been practicing so you can show him what you're made of at the Hunter Trial."

"And what gave you the right to tell my cousin anything about me?" Mary flashed, and I blinked in surprise. It was so unexpected coming from this usually timid English girl. "I – I thought –"

"That's your trouble Billie, you think too much and you always think you're right. From now on I'll fight my own battles, and you and your bossy boyfriend can stay away!"

The door slammed emphatically behind her and Paul and I were left outside it, gaping at each other in complete astonishment.

Chapter Nine

Paul recovered first. "She's very upset, Billie, please don't be offended. I'll talk to her."

He disappeared too, and I was left on the landing feeling a little upset myself. It didn't feel right hanging around there so I slowly made my way downstairs and was just about to leave when Paul came limping rapidly into the kitchen.

"Don't go," he begged. "Mary didn't mean what she said. She's just so wound up with everything."

"I don't blame her," I said with feeling. "She's had the worst few months I could imagine, but if she thinks Jack and I are interfering too much –"

"I don't." Mary appeared behind her cousin. "And I'm sorry I yelled at you. Paul told me everything you said, and I think it's brilliant that we're going to keep Longrigg after all."

"So do I." I smiled at her to show I wasn't sulking or anything. "But it means you won't need us any more – there's no need to go in for the Hunter Trial and –"

"Oh yes, there is!" Mary's chin came up defiantly. "I said

I was going to show Kyle Pritchard I'm not some snivelling little coward he can chase off, and show him I will."

"She's tougher than she looks," I said to Paul, and he seemed torn between admiration and concern as he put his arm around her.

"You will still help with Solace, won't you Billie?" His kindly face was worried again.

"Of course," I said, and as Jack appeared at the back door, added, "We're meeting here first thing tomorrow, aren't we Jack?"

"That's right," he agreed, but I noticed he was looking a bit anxious himself.

"What's the matter?" I asked him a short while later as we rode Gem and Cody back down the drive.

"Was Eddie in the house with Kyle and his father?" He was frowning.

"No, it was just the two Pritchards," I replied.

"That's odd. Eddie was driving the car when they left. I wonder where he was while they were inside?"

"Probably snooping around somewhere." I dismissed the thought. "Do you really think your beach idea is going to do the trick with Solace tomorrow?"

"Hope so. It's really down to Mary. She's got be absolutely determined."

The next day dawned bright and sunny, and we left Longrigg's gates in an optimistic mood. Mary enjoyed the ride across the hills but said she was missing seeing Maggie run beside her.

"Paul wasn't up when I left," she told us, "so I left her in the kitchen with the door shut."

"She'll be OK," I said. "When we get back we can take her with us to watch you do the lake jump."

"Oh, I do hope I can get Solace to do it." Mary's voice was fervent. The cliff top was looking particularly beautiful in the fresh morning light. Its crisp emerald turf was set against a background of clear blue sky and the sun glistened on the sea below us.

"What a gorgeous morning!" I stretched forward and gave my pony a hug. "Nothing can go wrong on a day like this."

Well, that was just asking for trouble, wasn't it?

Everything went fine at first. We had to ride down the side of a fairly steep cliff to get to the beach. It was more new territory for Mary and Solace, of course, but they managed very well, picking their way carefully between the rocks to arrive safely on the golden sand below.

"We'll take it very steadily," Jack said to Mary, "so that Solace can get used to the idea of being so close to the sea. What are you doing, Billie?"

I was, in fact, trying very hard to get Gem under control. He absolutely adores the beach and was eager to plunge straight into the shallows for our usual joyous canter through the waves.

"Sorry." I finally stopped him dancing around, and we walked sedately along the shoreline.

This stretch of beach is pretty remote and can't be reached by road so, aside from a few seagulls, we had it to ourselves. Later in the day a few sunbathers would arrive, having walked the long stretch from the nearest parking lot, but at this early hour it was all ours.

"It's so beautiful!" Mary breathed, her eyes shining as she looked across the sparkling bay.

Solace was rather funny, he was very interested in the waves lapping gently at the shore and stretched his neck down to inspect the lace-edged sea.

"That's good." Jack was watching in approval. "Let him take his time, and we'll gradually get him entering the water."

It was very pleasant riding up and down the length of the beach but it soon became clear that although Solace was enjoying himself he had absolutely no intention of putting his hooves in the sea. We tried everything we could think of, and at every pace. We'd walk, trot, and canter in single file, then in a group of three with Mary sandwiched between Jack and me, but as soon as Solace saw the waves flowing gently towards him he'd swerve away, often taking Jack and Cody with him. Since Solace loves to gallop we thought a race might do the trick, so we lined up enthusiastically. Mary held Solace back at first, and we could see him trying to push his nose ahead. Feeling sure he was fired up enough not to notice we were edging nearer the water, Jack and I gradually directed our ponies into the shallows. This time Solace thundered along with us but as soon as he felt the water on his feet he gave a huge lurch and carried Mary flat out to the warm, dry sand further up the beach. She stopped him with difficulty and turned back to face us, looking disappointed and wretched.

"It's no good." her voice trembled a little. "I just can't do it."

"Let me –" Jack was beginning to say when we heard a voice that sent a shiver scuttling down my spine.

"Hoy! Mary, Mary dumb and scary!"

"Kyle!" Jack looked around furiously. "How did he know we were here?"

"Ignore him," I said quickly, not wanting any more trouble. "Mary can get back at him when she tells Kyle he's not going to be living at Longrigg after all."

"You're right, Billie." Mary was looking up at the steep cliff face. "He's up there somewhere so he can't do anything to hurt us."

"Can you hear me, you little wimp?" With Kyle's loud, bullying tones she could hardly fail to, but she ignored him completely.

"I've got something of yours – look!"

Squinting against the sun, we all peered upwards. We could see the two horses, Kyle's showy, pure white Anglo Arab gleaming out against the dark coat of the big bay that Eddie was riding, but at first we couldn't make out what was being held out to show us.

Then Mary gave a horrified gasp and the color drained from her face. "Maggie! They've got Maggie!"

I still couldn't see clearly but I heard the familiar bark as the terrier responded to her owner's voice.

"Come on!" Jack was all action. "We'll get her Mary, don't worry."

He bounded off up the craggy path, pushing Cody at a speed we'd normally never use on the cliff ascent. I followed more cautiously on Gem. We reached the top in record time, and ahead of me, I could see Jack and Cody in hot pursuit of the white horse, who was galloping at a tremendous pace along the turf trail of the hills. I couldn't see Eddie on the bay horse but assumed he was further ahead and put my courageous pony into gallop to join in the chase. There was no chance of enjoying the beauty of the cliff top this time as we raced across the turf. Gem, as usual, did his best, his hooves pounding their four-time beat as he almost flew after the pursuing Cody. Cody and the Anglo Arab are faster, though, and I could see them drawing further ahead, until a faint roar of rage wafted back

to me and I saw Jack begin to slow his pony down, curving him in a semi-circle so that they were now cantering back towards me.

"Go back, Billie!" he was yelling. "It's a trick!"

By the time I'd managed to turn Gem, Jack and Cody had reached us and they cantered alongside.

"Why are you letting Kyle get away?" I shouted.

"It's not Kyle, that was Eddie we were chasing. They've swapped horses to fool us and Kyle is back there somewhere with Maggie."

I could see the anger in his face. "You go on." I knew our slower pace was holding him back. "He must have gone down to the beach by a different path."

Jack set Cody into gallop again and they surged ahead, reaching the cliff path several minutes before Gem and I did. I brought my pony to a halt on the top of the cliff and stared desperately down to see what was going on. Jack had already reached the beach and was galloping flat out along the sand again, this time chasing the heavier bay horse usually ridden by Eddie. I could just make out the rider and Jack was right – it was definitely Kyle who was trying to make his escape on the groom's horse. But where was Maggie? I couldn't see her and thought Kyle must be holding her in front of him. Then I heard Mary's voice and brought my gaze back to the beach below where she was shouting something. She was making no attempt to follow Jack and, for a moment, I couldn't understand why not, then I realized who she was calling to. There, several yards out to sea, was the Tibetan Terrier, huddled nervously on a rocky outcrop, waves breaking over her in huge drifts of spray as the tide came in.

"Maggie!" I started slithering rapidly down the cliff path, again taking the steep slope faster than I ever had.

I had to reach the shore and ride out to save the little dog before the incoming tide covered the rock and swept her into its depths. My eyes were fixed on the ground, trying to keep Gem safe as we hurtled downwards but, just as we touched down on the sand, I looked up and could hardly believe what I was seeing. Mary and Solace were surging through the waves, the water chest deep on the big horse as Mary drove him nearer and nearer the rocks. With one sweeping movement she bent down and scooped the soaked and frightened dog into her arms, setting her on the front of the saddle as she turned Solace and brought him, splashing gloriously through the shallows, as the three of them returned to the shore.

"Oh Mary!" I was nearly in tears. "You were fantastic! Is Maggie OK?"

"I think so." She slid off her horse and lifted Maggie onto the dry sand. The terrier was sopping wet, her thick coat plastered to her body. But, after several giant shakes that showered us all with sea water, she looked much better and licked Mary's hand lovingly.

"She's saying thank you." I dismounted too and gave the little dog a cuddle.

"It's Solace who should get the credit." Mary stood up and hugged her horse who now stood calmly at the edge of the sea, happily oblivious to the incoming tide as it lapped and swirled around him.

"What happened?" I was pretty sure I knew and when Mary said, "It was Kyle of course," I nodded.

"He came down to the beach as soon as Jack and I took off after the white horse?"

"Yes." She was pale, but clear-eyed and triumphant looking. "I followed you both but I was much slower.

Before I got half way up the cliff, I saw Kyle on the bay horse, coming down that other path over there. I could see he was carrying Maggie so I turned Solace round straight away and came back to the beach to confront him."

"Then what?" I was still stroking Maggie, noticing the way her collar sparkled against the cream and gray coat that was already starting to fluff out in the sun.

"Then he did a load of name calling, the usual stuff, and started teasing me about being too scared to ride Solace in the water."

"How did he know that?" I couldn't believe my ears.

"No idea, but he knew all right. He said if I stayed at Longrigg he'd make my life a misery so it would be better for me if I talked Paul into selling."

"Didn't you tell him his father isn't going to be able to buy the house?"

She took a deep breath. "Yes I did. I thought it might make him stop tormenting me and give Maggie back if he knew he'd got nothing to gain by scaring me anymore, but –" she bent down and cuddled the terrier so I wouldn't see the tears in her eyes.

"But it just made Kyle madder than ever and he took Maggie out to sea and dumped her," I said, hardly believing even Kyle could be so cruel.

Mary swallowed hard and said, "Yes. He – he rode the horse out into the sea, following that line of rocks until he reached the very last one. He even called out, quite casually over his shoulder, 'Too bad you can't get out here because when the tide comes in your dog will drown. Maybe that'll teach you not to mess with me!'"

"Oh, Mary!" I gave her a hug, and she smiled bravely.

"I was just going to wade or swim out on my own but I

90

thought I might not reach her in time. Instead I urged Solace forward with everything I've got. He wouldn't go at first but I knew we had to go into that water, and I was so determined he gave in and started walking into the sea. Once he was in he was fine and – well, you saw how deep he went and what a wonderful job he made of rescuing Maggie."

"And it was all down to you, Mary. You were terrific."

"Thanks Billie, and thanks for trying to get Maggie back too."

"I can't stand to think about what Kyle did to her," I said passionately, "but at least his father won't allow him to enter Saturday's Hunter Trial when we tell him about this."

"We can't say anything." She bit her lip. "Not until Paul has the money sorted, I told you."

"But…" I stared at her in disbelief. "Kyle knows he's not going to get Longrigg now. You told him so."

"He didn't believe her." Jack had come back along the beach and was walking Cody towards us. "He's such a liar himself he thought Mary made it up. I didn't stick it to him, at least not about that."

"What did you do?" I asked curiously, looking at the hard set of his jaw.

"Caught up with him, dragged him off Eddie's horse, and started teaching him another lesson." Jack smiled grimly. "I'd have made it a longer one but he started bawling like a big kid and told me I ought to get back to Mary and rescue her dog. I hadn't seen Maggie on the rock until then, I was so intent on chasing Kyle. When he told me what he'd done I left him and started galloping back, then I saw Mary ride Solace into the sea and knew Maggie was going to be OK. Bravo, Mary!"

"You said she had to be really determined to get Solace in there, didn't you?" I smiled at him,, and he grinned back in that devilish, heart-stopping way of his.

"I did, didn't I? Now you've got every chance of beating Kyle on Saturday, Mary. It'll be another lesson he won't forget."

"If only we'd solved the missing emerald mystery too." I couldn't stop thinking about it. "Then we'd be able to report Kyle and that creepy Eddie."

"It was probably Eddie's idea to kidnap Maggie and set up this morning's trick." Jack leaned over and squeezed my hand comfortingly. "I reckon he was keeping out of sight in the SUV yesterday and overheard us discussing Mary's problem with getting Solace into the water. That's how they knew we'd be here."

"I expect you're right," Mary said, lifting Maggie onto her saddle and climbing up behind her. "Let's get my poor little dog home, she's been through enough."

"Sure," I said. "And we can have one more try at looking for the Longrigg Emerald while we're there."

"OK," Jack said reluctantly. "But this is the last time, all right?"

We nodded and set off up the cliff, as the tide continued to come in, surging strongly towards the beach and completely covering the rock where Kyle had dumped Maggie just a short time before.

Chapter Ten

Although we were all in complete accord on the way back, there was a slight disagreement when we finally reached Longrigg House. Mary wanted to fuss around checking Maggie over and toweling her until she was thoroughly dry, but Jack insisted she should take Solace up to the lake and pop him over the jump while his successful debut into water was still fresh in his mind.

I looked at the stubborn expressions both of them were wearing and tried a little peace-making. "Jack's probably right, Mary. It would be a shame if you don't take advantage of what happened today. I'll stay here and look after Maggie. You won't be long, and I can start drying her while you're gone."

"Would you use my blow dryer then?" Mary didn't like it when Jack "bossed her about" as she put it, but she could see the sense in what he said.

"Of course I will." I quickly untacked Gem and left him with a haynet while I carried the still-damp terrier over to the house.

I had to hold on to her tightly to stop her running after her beloved Mary, but when I put her in her bed with a few biscuits she settled down and let me brush the tangles out of her coat as it dried. I took her collar off to get at the hair around her neck and had just about finished when she barked loudly and started wagging her feathery tail excitedly.

"Yes, it's me!" Mary ran into the kitchen and the little dog jumped straight into her arms. "Oh, she looks fine now. Thanks, Billie."

"You're welcome." I switched off the dryer. "How did you and Solace do?"

"Perfect." She hugged Maggie to her. "Absolutely perfect. He cleared the jump and landed in that lake as if it was the most natural thing in the world. Jack said to do it like that for the next couple of days, and we'll have no trouble at the competition. Your boyfriend's very bossy but he does seem to know what he's talking about."

"Great, good job." I was really pleased she'd accomplished the water jump at last. "Where's Jack now?"

"Taking care of the horses. He said to start our final search for the missing emerald, and he'd come along later."

"I'll bet he doesn't," I said. "Come on, are there any rooms we haven't searched yet?"

"I don't think so." Mary set Maggie down and put her collar back on. "There you are Mags, all beautiful again, my little gem."

"You can't call her a gem, that's my horse's name," I said teasingly.

She laughed. "Did you pick the name because he's such a treasure?"

I must have looked blank because she added, "You know, gem as in jewel."

"No," I said slowly. "It's Gem short for Gemini in his case, nothing to do with precious stones – but you've given me an idea."

"Really?" Mary looked at me eagerly. "What is it?"

I shook my head. "I haven't thought it through yet. I'll tell you when I have."

"Oh, OK." Mary led us through to the paneled hall. "Shall we have one more try in here and see if there's a secret hideaway my great-uncle could have used?"

I was pretty bored at the prospect, since we seemed to have crawled over every inch of the house already. But I helped her again, while all the time the faint idea buzzed gently in my brain. It was ages before Jack came in to join us and he was obviously not wild about the "last hunt". We kept at it for over an hour, though we were glad to stop when we heard Paul arrive back.

"You've got Maggie," he greeted us with relief. "I let her out by mistake, opened the back door, and she was off like a rocket. I thought she'd go chasing after you. Did she find you OK?"

"Not exactly." Mary was still reluctant to tell Paul about Kyle's latest horror. "Paul, did the bank lend you the money you need?"

"Not yet." He looked glum. "I think they will, but there are a lot of formalities. To start with, there has to be a survey done on this place, so it's going to take a few days."

"We'll tell you about our morning when it's all settled then." Mary gave Jack and I a firm look. "And I don't think you should report Kyle and his groom to Mr. Pritchard until then either."

I opened my mouth to disagree but she shot me a fierce glance, so I obediently shut it again. Jack and I left soon

afterwards, riding our hardworking ponies very gently back to the yard after their adventurous time on the cliff top and beach.

"Mary's changed a lot, hasn't she?" I remarked as we plodded side-by-side. "She wouldn't say 'boo' to a goose when we first met her but she stands up for herself really well now."

"It's helped her riding too," Jack agreed. "She's much more positive, and she's stopped that irritating thing she used to do with her stirrup leathers and girth."

"Let's hope it all pays off, and she does really well at Saturday's competition. It would be terrible if Kyle won the cup."

"He'll want to win it more than ever after his failure this morning," Jack said.

"I wish Mary had told Paul about it," I said, shuddering at the memory of little Maggie huddled on that sea-swept rock.

"I think she's right not to stir up more trouble until the money's sorted out," Jack said thoughtfully. "It would be a disaster if Paul finally called the deal off and then found he had to sell Longrigg after all."

"He's not going to sell." I said emphatically. "I had an idea earlier on Jack, an idea about the missing emerald —"

"Oh no, not more searching!" He scowled at me. "Forget it Billie, let's spend the next two days getting ready for the Hunter Trial instead."

It was a pain the way he wouldn't listen, but although I spent most of our time together preparing for the contest as he said, it didn't stop me puzzling the mystery through. It all hinged on a name, we knew that and I'd suddenly become aware just how many different significant names

there were. I spent the evening before the trial looking up all the ones I'd thought of. Now I was absolutely sure I had the answer, but I decided to wait to tell everyone until after we'd all competed.

The day of the trial was perfect, dry and warm with a little hazy cloud and a gently cooling breeze. We met up with Mary at the grounds and collected our numbers together. Mary, surprisingly, was less nervous than I thought she'd be.

"My legs feel like mashed potatoes," I told her, "all soft and soggy, and I haven't just got butterflies in my tummy, more like a crowd of bats swooping around in there."

"I'm not too bad." She certainly looked pretty cool, I had to admit. "I think it's because I'm so psyched up to beat Kyle."

"It's your way of getting back at him, isn't it?" I admired her determination. "Come on, let's warm up, I'm the first of us three to go."

The course, which we'd walked earlier, looked great I had to say, despite my nerves. There were 21 jumps, ranging from simple bales and tires to a hanging log and double bounce, plus, of course, the water. Mary had inspected that one really carefully and was sure Solace would handle it well.

"Thanks to you and Jack, he's popping in and out of our lake as though he's done it all his life," she told me. "And he'll love all the other fences as well."

I didn't tell her I wasn't quite as confident myself but, as soon as my number was called and I went off through the start, I felt better. Gem took the bales, shark's teeth, drop, and gate perfectly and, by the time we approached the big jump, I was really enjoying myself. We weren't going at a

great rate and I knew our time could be beaten, but I concentrated on getting over everything safely. There was a choice of two routes at some of the jump combinations. You could choose the more difficult way, which was quicker, or the slower, easier way and I decided on the harder jump each time, because Gem, was jumping so well. We soared over the number 21 obstacle, a very attractive (and big!) trough of flowers and galloped strongly to the finish, with shouts of congratulations from Jack, Mary, and lots of other friends ringing happily in our ears. Despite our steady pace we were within the time limit so we didn't pick up any penalty points, and one of the stewards told me I'd set the standard that everyone else would now have to beat.

I was thrilled at the way my wonderful pony had gone around and stuffed about a million carrots into him while he cooled off. We watched and listened to the next few contestants. We couldn't see the whole course, which was cleverly planned in a series of serpentine curves around the grounds, but there was a loudspeaker system broadcasting a detailed commentary. It soon became clear that there was no bogey fence which would trip everyone up, but it wasn't as straightforward and easy as my clever Gem had made it look either. Someone got 20 penalties for neglecting to replace a slip rail and there were several who had one or even two refusals when they rushed their horses through the "quick" route. I thought I'd done a fairly slow time but one person on a placid-looking cob plodded around, looking, as Jack put it, like they were out for a countryside ramble instead of a Hunter Trial, and ended up with 40 penalties plus another 40 time ones.

Jack was next to go after him, and he and Cody shot through the start like a bullet from a gun. There was just no

comparison – the pair of them flew around the first part of that course in what must have been an unbeatable time – until disaster struck. Obstacle number 14 was the large tiger trap to the left of number 15, the knockdown rail. Jack said later that he'd been so carried away at that point with sheer speed and competitiveness that, despite the steward's flag, he didn't even realize he'd taken the wrong route until Cody was galloping away from the tiger trap which he'd taken after the rail. As in most competitions, jumping obstacles in the wrong order meant elimination, and poor Jack was absolutely wrecked.

"I can't believe I could be so stupid!" he raged. "Whatever you do, Mary, don't make the same mistake I just did."

"Right." Mary, psyched up and ready to go, was very pale now. "I wish Kyle had already done his round. I don't know how fast I have to go to beat him."

"He'll be fast," Jack said with grim certainty. "At the moment Billie and Gem are still in the lead. Nobody else has completed the course without picking up penalties."

"And you and Solace can beat our time and Kyle Pritchard's." I patted her back encouragingly. "I really want you to do it."

"Thanks, Billie." She gave me a grateful smile and started walking Solace to the start.

Jack and I left Cody and Gem with some friends from our yard and sprinted off to get a good viewing spot near the water.

"I'm sure she'll do fine." I had my fingers crossed for luck. "And if Solace takes this jump well, he'll be in with every chance of winning."

We couldn't see the start or the first few fences from the viewing area around the water but we listened intently to

the commentary and knew Mary was doing really well, galloping her talented black horse confidently to each obstacle. They'd just negotiated the knock-down rail and, at last, came into view as they approached the water.

"She's going at a great pace." Jack almost forgot his annoyance at messing up his own round. "If she keeps going with that same impulsion Solace will have the confidence to take the jump into the water."

We held our breath and watched as they came nearer and nearer the fence. It wasn't very big, but it was solidly built and there was a slight drop, meaning the horse would land knee-deep in the pond on the other side. For one horrible moment it looked as though Solace hesitated, and I clutched Jack in fright. He put his arm comfortingly round me and, as he did, Solace took off, soaring athletically to clear the fence easily. He landed smoothly and surged powerfully through the water and out the other side. Jack, still with his arm around my waist, and I stood and gazed after the black horse as he galloped up the hill and took jump number 17, the hay rack, easily in his stride. There were only four more to go and we waited expectantly, leaping in the air when the commentator announced that Mary and Solace had finished the course with no penalties and had knocked several seconds off the former leader's time.

"Why are we cheering?" Jack gave me another hug. "You're the leader she's just beaten!"

"I don't mind in the least coming in second to Mary." I really meant it. "Now we've just got to hope that Kyle doesn't go even faster."

"Oh hang on −" Jack stopped jumping around. "Listen, Kyle is riding now, I've just heard the loudspeaker say he's cleared number four."

It was too late to run back and get a better view of the course so we stood there, waiting for the beautiful white Anglo Arab to gallop into view, and were soon joined by a breathless Mary.

"I left Solace with Paul," she said. "He told me you were here cheering me on. Wasn't Solace just wonderful?"

"You were both fantastic." I hugged her. "And hopefully in an unbeatable time too!"

"Don't speak too soon," Jack warned, frowning as he listened to the commentary. "Kyle is going even faster and so far his horse hasn't put a foot wrong."

All three of us listened intently as the loudspeaker crackled, "Kyle Pritchard is now approaching number 16, the water." The Anglo Arab was almost upon us, stretching every muscle as Kyle drove him relentlessly towards the fence at the edge of the pond. We could see exactly what Jack meant about Kyle's riding. Even though the magnificent horse was giving his all, Kyle continually kicked and lashed him, trying to get even more speed. They soared over the jump perfectly but, even so, Kyle still lost his balance and jabbed his poor mount painfully in the mouth while he yanked on the reins to regain his seat.

As Jack said, at that point it was as if the white horse decided he'd finally had enough. Instead of heading for dry land he suddenly stopped dead and bent his neck sharply. Kyle, still clumsily thumping around on his back, was taken completely by surprise and slid, still scrabbling wildly, head first into the pond. As he emerged, spluttering furiously to get rid of the mud and pond weeds that clung to his face, his horse surged forward, knocking him flat again. The crowd roared with laughter as they watched Kyle

101

floundering once more in the water, and many of them cheered as the Anglo Arab cantered smoothly away.

"Now that will really hurt!" Jack was delighted. "Kyle does hate to be laughed at."

"Everyone could see he deserved it." I couldn't stop giggling. There was a wonderful poetic justice in the way Kyle had lost.

And now that the excitement was over I could tell my friends that I had some more, even greater, news. After all that thinking and research I had finally solved the mystery of the missing emerald!

Chapter Eleven

Jack, as usual when it came to my brain power, was not impressed.

"Oh, come on Billie, we don't need to ruin the day with another one of your half-baked ideas."

I was offended. "Actually there was nothing half-baked about my original thinking," I told him with great dignity. "The idea was just fine but I hadn't thought it through enough."

"Oooh Billie, I can't wait!" Mary was much more excited, I'm pleased to say. "It will just make everything perfect if we find the emerald and Paul doesn't have to mortgage Longrigg. He hasn't said much but I know he's hating the thought. Tell us now, go on."

"No." I was feeling quite annoyed with Jack. I knew he was still irritated with himself at getting eliminated and was taking his bad temper out on me. I wasn't going to let him get away with it. "We'll celebrate the presentation of the winner's cup, and I'll come back with you to Longrigg afterwards and show you the solution then." I turned my

back deliberately on Jack to show he wasn't included, and he almost ran up the hill after me.

"Don't be mad at me, Billie," he said, his dark eyes pleading.

"Why not?" I said huffily. "You obviously think I'm some sort of idiot."

"No I don't, I think you're brilliant."

"Oh yeah?" I was still walking away.

"Yes I do. And besides clever, you're kind and generous and – and –"

"And what?" I turned to face him.

"And really, really pretty." He'd never told me that before and looked so gorgeous when he said it I just couldn't resist.

I shook out my long, dark hair and smiled at him. "So you'll come back to Longrigg with me?"

"You know I will." He took my hand briefly, and I felt that wonderful warm glow spread through me.

The presentation was beautiful. Everyone made such a fuss of Mary and of me, too. We were the only competitors to have completed the course without incurring any penalties and the judge who was giving out the prizes was very complimentary. Not surprisingly there was no sign of Kyle, who had obviously slunk home to wash off the pond mud and slime. Paul was there of course, looking immensely proud of Mary. She told him about the breakthrough I thought I'd made with the missing emerald mystery.

I could tell Paul was thinking along the same lines as Jack but at least he was polite.

"Er – wonderful," he said, and Mary tugged his hand impatiently.

"I can't wait to get back to Longrigg – Billie's going to show us where the emerald is!"

Mary and I were full of hope and high spirits on the way back. I had just a moment of doubt as we rode up the now-familiar long drive to the stable yard. Wouldn't it be awful if I was wrong, if "using my brain" had only ended up in another failure! Mary looked so happy, completely different from the nervous, tearful girl of just a few weeks ago, and I would hate to make her sad again. I pulled myself together. I had to believe in my theory and, if the worst happened and I was wrong, at least this time didn't involve hours of crawling around behind paintings and paneled walls. We settled the horses and joined Paul in the drawing room. He had a tray of cold drinks and we toasted our success in the Hunter Trial first and then everyone's eyes turned towards me.

"It was something Mary said that gave me this idea," I began, a little nervously. "I'd been drying Maggie after that beast Kyle dumped her in the sea –"

"He did what?" I had never heard the mild, gentle Paul roar like that.

"I'll tell you all about that in a minute." Mary was tense with anticipation. "Go on, Billie."

"I'd taken her collar off," I started again and this time was interrupted by a groan from Jack.

"You're not going to tell us you think the emerald is one of the jewels in Maggie's collar? I told you I've seen that sparkly kind lots of times, they sell them in the local pet shop."

"That's where I bought the one that Maggie's wearing," Paul joined in, and I sighed deeply.

"Let Billie tell us properly," Mary begged the other two.

"Thank you, Mary. As I was saying, I'd taken her collar off and when you put it back on you called her your little gem. You told me you thought I'd called my pony Gem because he's such a jewel and that got me thinking. There are lots of different words for a jewel, aren't there? – gemstone, precious stone, treasure, brilliant, as well as all the words for specific jewels like diamond, ruby or sapphire. And those, in turn, have other descriptions, diamond being a form of carbon for instance whereas ruby is a precious variety of corundum."

"OK, OK." Jack was grinning at me fondly. "We can tell you've been using your brains, Billie. Where's all this taking us?"

"You can see from what I told you that I did a lot of research." I was starting to enjoy myself now that I had their attention. "I was sure my original idea was along the right lines, we know that the clue Paul's father mentioned existed in the name of somebody or something. But it wasn't the name 'Jewel' as we found out, so I investigated other possibilities. It was when I looked up the word 'emerald' I knew at once where he'd hidden it."

I paused for effect, and they all looked suitably baffled.

"Well, go on!" Jack pulled my long braid gently. "What's another name for an emerald?"

"Could I have that dictionary from the shelf, Paul?" I took it from him and turned the pages. "Here we are – emerald – a green transparent variety highly valued as a gem."

"Gem again," Mary said, bewildered. "Variety of what?"

I took a deep breath and said dramatically, "A variety of beryl."

"Beryl," Paul repeated blankly, then did a double take.

"My mother's dog, the first Tibetan Terrier, was called Beryl!"

"Exactly." I didn't say "I rest my case", though I felt like it.

"I hope you don't mean we have to start poking around all the paintings of the dog now?" Jack said in disgust.

"Of course not," I said. "It's obvious where the emerald is hidden, isn't it? Look Paul, you do the next part – I hate that room, and I'd rather you brought it here to us."

"Brought what here?" He hadn't worked it out either, but Mary gave a sudden excited squeak.

"I know what she means. Ooh, come on Paul, I'll show you!"

She grabbed his hand and rushed him out of the room.

"Where are they going?" Jack still looked baffled.

"To the trophy room." I looked at him. "Doesn't that give you the answer?"

He shook his head, and I said slowly and clearly, "to get the collar. The collar that the stuffed dog Beryl is wearing. Paul's father would probably think it fitting that the emerald he bought for his beloved wife should be hidden in the collar worn by the little dog she adored so much."

"No way! I knew he was eccentric but –" Jack's words were drowned by a loud shriek from Mary.

She came running into the room, light flashing from the glittering, sparkling collar she was holding high in her hand. Maggie, who'd naturally followed her to and from the trophy room, gave a loud bark and jumped up at her, obviously joining in the excitement.

"Billie, look, look!" Mary was almost babbling. "We took off Sukey's first, 'cause you can't see which dog is which underneath all that hair, then we saw it had her name

on the little tag. As soon as Paul undid the one belonging to Beryl he knew you were right."

"It's much heavier," Paul explained, following her in with a huge, delighted smile all over his face. "My father must have removed three or four of the fake jewels and fixed the Longrigg emerald in their place. He'd have liked it that Beryl's name meant emerald – maybe that's why he bought the jewel all those years ago."

"Maybe," I agreed, thinking privately that we'd never work out the thinking behind anything Paul's father had done.

"Whatever he meant, we've found the missing jewel at last!" Mary hugged and hugged me. "It means Paul's plans can go ahead, he can set up this summer school and I can stay here for ever and ever if I want."

"You might just get a bit more trouble from Kyle," Jack pointed out. "Not that I want to spoil the moment but –"

"I'd almost forgotten, Kyle," Mary stopped hugging me and turned to Paul, her face serious. "Now I can tell you about the other morning and what Kyle did to Maggie."

It took a while but between us we told Paul about Kyle and Eddie's latest dirty trick, and I could see how shocked and angry he was. Up until then I'd thought he was rather a weak character, amiable and nice enough, but too immersed in his "artsy" world to deal with life on a practical level. I was proved wrong, though, over the next couple of days as Paul paid a visit to Mr. Pritchard, arranged the valuation and sale of the emerald and employed plumbers and decorators to finish the house improvements. We didn't accompany him on any of these missions, but we saw the results very clearly. Once money was available, the house spoke for itself and became more habitable and welcoming every day.

The situation with Kyle was even more dramatic. Mr. Pritchard, shocked beyond belief at his son's behavior, was swift to try and set things right. His first action was to fire the evil Eddie and the next was to insist his son sold his horses – Paul had pointed out how badly they were being treated. Best of all, Mr. Pritchard decided that he and Kyle would move away from the area to clear the bad name Kyle created for himself. He told Paul he intended to spend more time with his son and help him become a decent member of society.

"He's got his work cut out for him!" Jack said cynically, but the kind-hearted Paul was more hopeful.

"It makes all the difference having family who care about you," he said, looking fondly at Mary, who smiled back immediately. "We know that, don't we Mary, so there's hope yet for Kyle."

I thought it was great to see them looking so happy and life did, indeed, look perfect. Jack and I were closer than ever too – and he told me that he'd never doubt my brainpower again.

"Because," he explained, hugging me exuberantly, "You were the one who finally solved the mystery of the missing emerald!"

I hugged him back, feeling incredibly happy myself. "Thanks, pardner! But I can't take all the credit, can I? The reason I worked it out was because I'm lucky enough to own a horse called Gem!"